Unscheduled Departures:
THE ASYLUM ANTHOLOGY
OF SHORT FICTION

Unscheduled Departures

THE ASYLUM ANTHOLOGY OF SHORT FICTION

Edited by Greg Boyd

Santa Maria / Asylum Arts / 1991

Acknowledgements

Library of Congress Catalogue Number 90-086266
ISBN No. 1-878580-11-6

Cover illustration by Bruce Salter

These stories originally appeared in ASYLUM magazine between the years 1985 and 1991. All appear again here with the kind permission of their authors. Some of these stories have since been reprinted as part of larger collections of an author's work and appear here with their publishers' kind permission: "Oswald's Secret" from *Assassination Rhapsody*, Semiotext[e]: Foreign Agents Series: New York, 1989, © Derek Pell and Autonomedia; "Equus Caballus" from *The Beak Doctor*, Europa Media, 1987; "Flying Lessons" from *After Uelsmann*, Bottom Dog Press, 1988; "Sarah Bernhardt's Leg" from *Ambit 112*; "Bo" from *All Gone: 18 Short Stories*, The Johns Hopkins University Press, Baltimore/London, 1990, pp. 128-136; "I Always Carry A Gun" from *Another Perfect Murder*, Asylum Arts, 1991; "Under the Eaves" from *Water & Power*, Asylum Arts, 1991; "These Words" from *The Manniken Cypher*, Bomb Shelter Props, 1989; "Oh How Time Flies" from *The Plantings*, The Runaway Spoon Press, 1989.

This anthology is published concurrently as Volume 7, numbers 1 & 2 of ASYLUM.

Asylum Arts Publishing
P. O. Box 6203
Santa Maria, CA 93456

Contents

These Words

Thomas Wiloch

Sometimes I wonder about who reads these words. I know where the words come from. They start inside of me, at a point inside my head just behind my eyes and between my ears. That's the point where, when I want to make words and don't want to use my mouth to form them, I am able to "say" the words without their being heard by anyone but me.

That's where these words come from.

Where they go I can only guess at this point. I will send them to a magazine that likes to print words of this kind, words that come from inside somebody and are written down on paper, are later typed up neatly on clean white sheets, and mailed out in an envelope. There are magazines out there that print such words. And people who buy those magaznes because they like to read words like these.

It is a December night in the late 1980's as I write these words in a spiral notebook in my house. When I go to the office tomorrow, I will type these words during lunchtime and mail them out to a magazine. They will be read by the magazine's editor, and by his typesetter and his printer, and eventually, when the magazine appears in a few month's time, by people who buy the magazine. Perhaps you are one of those magazine buyers who are reading these words. If so, hello.

But it doesn't stop there. It goes on. That magazine will still exist long after the last copy is sold. It will be on shelves and in boxes and stuffed into desk drawers all over the world. Years from now, when the magazine buyer has long forgotten that magazine, someone else can run across it, and leaf through the pages, and stop at this page, and read these words.

It even continues. Maybe I will gather these words together with other words I have written. I will call that big group of words a book. There are publishers who print books filled with words like these, and there are people who buy and read such books too. Perhaps that is who you are, a person who has bought that hypothetical book of the future. If so, hello.

After a time that book will go out of print. Years later, a stray copy of that book could be on a shelf in a secondhand bookstore. A customer is browsing, scanning the book titles for something of interest, something to kill a little of his time. He sees a book and glances through it, stops at these words, and reads them.

Maybe it is some time in the middle of the next century, in a store in a distant city, and this book browser is standing in an aisle with a book in his hands (rather dusty and battered by then!), and he is reading these words silently to himself, pronouncing these words with that little voice he has inside his head, behind his eyes and between his ears. And he wonders to himself, who is the guy who wrote these words? What was he like? What was his purpose in writing these words?

If that is you, a dead man says hello. What's the next century like?

And so these words will continue to live, reincarnating afresh within each new person who reads them, all of us strangers to one another, but sharing the secret of these words.

Conte

Robert Fagan

To have a wife who is beautiful is good. To have a wife who is amorous is also good. But to have a beautiful wife who loves other men, when you are poor and other men are rich, is the best thing in the world. I count myself lucky, except for moments like these, when I have to make the arrangements. Even a man of the world is not always at ease; and, as I stood before the water closets in the dark subbasement of the Folies-Bergère, I wondered about my wife's strange description of what was not to be the usual fop. Indeed, she had warned me he was a giant of a man. And now the light from the doorway above was blocked. I murmured, "Bon soir," but the giant began to descend in silence.

Certainly he was tall. But he seemed to be less than six feet even with boots on, and they had high heels and thick soles. So he was not tall. His incredible mane of black hair merely gave him a massive and stately appearance. With a military haircut he might have seemed small. And from another vantage point—if I were not standing at the bottom of the stairs and he above—he would surely appear short. In fact, his head did not come near the ceiling above the top step, where tall men like myself almost have to stoop. So the boots and the wig were an obvious subterfuge; they lost their power to disguise his smallness as he descended further—and on the last three steps became lower than my forehead, lower than my chin, as low as my chest.

This was too much, or rather too little. My wife, as usual, was not to be trusted. I had been prepared to back up against the wall of WC's, fold my arms together firmly, and give myself all the stature a man-to-man talk demands. Now I didn't know what to do with my arms. They were hanging down: long, apelike, monstrous, a possible embarrassment to my miniature guest. I hid them behind me. But then he reached out his hand, and I had to extend my own vast paw. I pulled it back immediately, before it could crush him.

His tiny eyes crinkled in an infinitesimal smile. I backed further away, bemused. How would I begin the discussion of money? My wife's consideration of this dwarf as a candidate for her bed might be an act of charity. That always difficult subject—the value of my wife's body—might not be broached. Or did he have a rich father who was desperate to find his son companionship? But his smiling face was hardly young. In fact, it was hardly smiling: The creases were permanent. And the eyes were tired, overlapped by sagging brows and puffed cheeks that formed the cynical sleepy smile that was not a smile, only the utmost in fatigue. This was no youth who had yet to attain his full height, but rather someone whose body had shrunk, year after year, inch by inch—someone who perhaps had once not been a dwarf.

What could my voluptuous wife want with this relic of another age? Yet this *ancien régime* mannequin might once have been a duke or a general or a banker. Certainly, an aura of authority remained on the immobile face under the black wig. The black boots held a man who was impervious, who had deigned to extend his hand, but otherwise had hardly noticed me. But now his eyes trapped mine. He spoke.

"Your wife is at my country house. She will be one of my servants, one of my small things, not quite one of my little rococo shepherdesses. Rather an indoor fixture, a maid to hold the towel over me when I rise from my bath, or something on a cold winter night to be added to the blankets on my bed. She tells me you are fond of her. I must emphasize that not only can you not see or communicate with her again, but you are not even to think of her. She does not exist for you, she has never existed for you, she will never exist for you. If you dream of her, it will not be the real her. If there is any resemblance to her in what you dream, you will wake sweating, vomiting, terrified, stupefied—until you turn on the light and think of practical things. Here now, in my generosity, in my tolerance and beneficence for the trivia that must add up to a world, here are some small things."

I saw and heard the tiny gold coins scatter over the filthy, unevenly paved floor. They would be caught between the jagged, ancient stones and disappear into the earth. My hands moved like a magician's, as I crawled in an ever-widening circle, grasping everything. Nothing escaped me. My hands were golden in the dark empty room.

But it must be the intermission. Men are crowding in. I'm

actually in the State Theatre at Lincoln Center.

To disenchant you further, I am not a pimp, but a well-known critic of the arts. In fact, I have exaggerated and grossly ornamented everything. Indeed, I could have given you a million versions of the same meeting. There is only one thing I cannot tell you: that in my story there is no resemblance to persons either living or dead.

The Steeplejack

John Richards

They need a steeplejack.

Right. That's terrific. I can see you with your legs wrapped around a steeple, dabbing paint or polishing the brass shingles or whatever it is they do up there.

Do you think I'd make a good steeplejack?

Oh, sure. With your mind, your brilliant mind, your IQ, your SAT score, your experience as a safety patrol girl, Junior Achievement, you can do it. With adequate training. A patient boss. A good ladder.

You don't think I can handle it.

Well, of course you can. Splendidly. You're agile as a spider. A regular monkey. But that's pretty athletic stuff. Isn't there something more in line with who you are?

Who am I? A gyno? Should I found Dustmops, Incorporated, be a maid, or a meter maid, or a brain surgeon, a tree surgeon, a sturgeon fisherman? Who am I?

I don't know.

I want to do something different. I want to be different. I want something exciting.

Have you considered Big Time Wrestling?

I want to be a steeplejack.

Last time I asked you to knock cobwebs off the ceiling you got a nosebleed standing on the chair.

Think of the views, views of the city in every direction, the buildings, the housetops shadowed with trees, and off in the distance, the countryside, white fences running up and down hillsides, little cows, little sheep dotting the landscape, the storms billowing on the horizon, traffic wiggling below, and the sky, being up there where I can touch it, put my hand right into it for once, where it can't get away, airplanes buzzing around my ears, feeling how King Kong felt, but the planes friendly, pilots nodding, maybe tipping their wings, helicopter pilots, traffic report copters stopping to chat with me between reports, me hanging onto the steeple, strapped to it with a thick leather belt, thick as a barber's strop, holding me firmly against the steeple, sharing lunch with the copter pilots, perhaps, or throwing scraps of bread from my sandwich into the air and watching them plummet toward the upturned faces of pedestrians, but the birds, that have become my friends, swoop down and snip the bread from the air, in the nick of time, just before the crusts drop into the open mouths of those looking up at me, and me, laughing with delight, with joy, with eyes shining, with tears the wind, the strong high wind has forced out of the corners of my eyes.

Honey, birds won't be pals up there. Didn't Alfred Hitchcock do something about this?

Of course they will, how can they help it? I'm up there, a visitor, a friendly face, hanging onto a narrrowing needle, in their country, oh, the prospect of it, every day, standing at the foot of a church, looking up, and then with ropes and pulleys, lassoing the gutter and outcroppings on the building, climbing up, using my legs and arms, pulling with all my might, dragging up a bucket of tools, up the face of the church, always climbing toward the cross at the top, every day, higher, until I can hold the cross at the top in my hands, lay my head at the foot of the cross, blessed art the steeplejacks!

But you're afraid of heights, for heaven sakes.

Of course I am.

Those heights, the kind of heights you're referring to. The stairwell in a tall building, the stairs spiraling down, tier after tier, without relief, an abyss, darkness. That's a typical height. A common height. I should be afraid of that. And I am. My stomach flutters. I spin. Swoon. I get the willies. Don't you? Or from high atop a kitchen chair looking down at the harsh kitchen tiles, nothing but blank white ceiling above and below cold, clean floor. I can feel my bones crack when I glance down, the thud of flesh, blood pooling in my caved-in cranium, my fading eyes staring blindly at that blight, the bulb in the ceiling, where's the redemption, why'd I climb on that chair in the first place? Or from an airplane window. Looking out I have every reason to voice my terror. My hands clutch the knitting on your sweater because of the absolute loneliness, careening through the air with nothing under my seat besides a seat, nothing tying me to the earth. I might as well be a chip of stone hurled by a child into the night, sailing through nothing to who knows what? What's happened to the earth while I'm up there, maybe it's gotten soft, weepy from missing me. And when the plane settles down on it, the whole ship will sink into the earth like into a wet, hot marshmallow and be swallowed, or what if angry at the way I abandoned it, the earth dodges this way and that as the pilot swerves to find the runway, the earth in a hideous game of tag, scoots out from beneath the plane and we whistle along touching nothing until we're out of fuel and just drop into the black oblivion of space because the earth is unforgiving, a jealous lover that must be touched and held. Naturally I'm afraid of heights like that, falls like that. But steeples, just think, these are blissful heights.

You were such a sweet child. I thought you'd be a ballerina.

I'll pirouette on the tip of the cathedral spire.

What about your hair?

No comb will ever untangle it.

People will look up your dress!!

I'll be too high to hear their filthy snickering.

What about your father?

He's sweet. He cares. He'll close his eyes.

Honey!

No, I'll see him at a stoplight on his way home from work. I'll write an affectionate message on a scrap of paper, fold it into a paper airplane and send it aloft. It'll land on the hood of his car. My daughter, the one way up there, in the stratosphere, that's her, he'll think, saying hello.

What if something happens to your father or me during the day, when you're working, let's say an aneurism, or a violent attack of sneezing, you know, his lights, or my lights, go out for no reason, how can we reach you? What telephone?

The church choir. Tell the master to sing the message, it'll reverberate in that gothic vault, I'll hear, I'll feel it in my hands because the wood beneath my palms will quiver with it.

I don't know, dear, I don't know, I don't know what we expected of you, after high school, after your BA, your MA, your PhD, your Post Doc, but, yes, I feel a little misled, honey, maybe we should have guessed when you studied the trapeze. We expected something different.

This is different.

Have you considered anything else?

Laundress in Paris, milkman to the pope, queen of a Nevada

cathouse, old crone, long distance telephone, I thought for a long time I wanted to be a lamp then a rug, then a yellow spaniel in a muddy field....

Well, at least you won't be a fireman.

Only when the spire is on fire.

I see. So. When's the interview?

It was.

Dare I? Did you? How?

Let's keep our fingers crossed.

The Gift

Celestine Frost

The pig, the Royal Himalayan peccary, sent you by Mrs. G. K. Hamilton of Witchita who enjoyed the delicacy here and thought of you, should be arriving soon. It weighs 900 pounds. In order not to be the victim of this gift, you must kill it at once and roast it in a pit of hot ashes.

Customarily, there are one thousand guests and festive music. So if you cannot find sufficient family and friends, summon strangers and tell them to eat fast and greedily.

This will leave you bones to make a bed (where the thousand strangers slept in pork), a royal bed of pigbone, true to Himalayan custom where (the land long barren of trees) every part of a slain animal is used, and pigbone, cut in planks, is blond as tulipwood (though at first it will be wet, red with clinging ligaments and filled with marrow).

We suggest that it be carved like ivory into a lacy headboard (fashioning, as we do, an ornate luxury from bare essentials), with thick pineapple posts supporting a broad canopy and velvet curtains; that the bed be set upon a platform, that the double doors beside it open on a grassy, rolling plain where, in the distance, and visible in clear weather, you can see the mountains, the high one rising above them all, king of the world!

We believe the sight of mountains will cleanse you of the glut of hogflesh and rice wine, suggest that on awakening, you rise, throw open the tall doors and, stepping out, set off across the plains!

This bed-kit comes to you from the best Tibetan pig-farm. It is fattened on the lower slopes of the incomparable mountains for our special customers. Supply limited. Place your order now.

Sarah Bernhardt's Leg

Kirby Olson

> *after David Kirby's title of the same name, and seeing Bernhardt's statue near the Parc Monceau in Paris on April 1, 1987.*

Nearly everyone is familiar with the story of Sarah Bernhardt's career as a Parisian actress, both before and after the amputation of her leg. What most people don't know, but which very old Parisians can still tell you, is the story of the separate career of her leg after the operation. An elderly man in a darkened bistro remembered being knocked dead by the hilarious antics of this leg in the clubs of Montmartre just after the first World War. It danced wildly, gaily, like Ray Bolger, or with the sweet grace of Fred Astaire. Playing Hamlet, during the famous "To be or not to be" scene it mimed the action so well that the entire, cynical Montmartre crowd was in tears. If he hadn't seen it himself, he said, he'd have thought someone was pulling his leg. The topper is, the old fellow said, that the leg became even more famous than Sarah Bernhardt herself. For every offer of marriage that Bernhardt received, her leg received three. Everyone jammed in to see it interpret the latest rag-time hit, or play a dramatic role, or sometimes even do parodies of whatever Sarah Bernhardt was currently playing. Finally, it opened at the Trocadero and Sarah Bernhardt came to see it perform a medley of its greatest successes. Her own career was suddenly stumbling due to her leg, and, enraged by the standing ovation her leg received, she went on stage, pretending to simply want to take a bow with it. She started trying to kick her leg, but kept falling down. It danced around her, trying to tease her and succeeding. Finally, she got a hold of it and smashed it repeatedly against the hard wood floor. The audience booed and screamed, "Murder!" The leg was so badly shaken by this incident that it could never perform again. It finally died, penniless, in a sordid little hotel on the Left Bank. Sarah Bernhardt was excused for this crime of passion, as great artists often are in France, and went on to new heights in drama—her crime forgotten by all but the few who remained attached to her leg.

Parable

Bruce Craven

There once was a man who owned gallons and gallons of little angels. He kept them pickled in casks made of the finest onyx, tops of intricately-patterned crystal. On special days he would dismiss his staff and with careful movements of anticipation, rustle down the twirling granite stairs and unlatch the doors to the secret chambers, a tremolo of pattering silk slippers announcing his arrival.

But nothing moved as the man hopped from cask to cask, wiping the crystal free of dust and peering in at the figurines that bobbed face-down, wings yellowing in vinegar.

On certain rare occasions the man's passions would arouse within him and he would tip the casks up onto their edge, jostling them. If only I could see their little faces! he would think, If only they'd look up! And then sometimes the man would cry, tasting salt at the back of his throat, wishing that he did not fit his fine clothes so well. But knowing that he did and being sorry.

And so it came to pass that when the bells of the town rang, announcing a national holiday of obscure origin, the man told his servants to take a week or two off. You know, really relax: cashing their checks with a wink, slicking their hair with lilac perfume. They whistled their merry way out the sunsplashed halls and down the path.

The man was relieved and went to fix himself a tonic of imported nectar. At least now I will have some time to myself, he thought. But passing the stairway of twirling granite, he felt the familiar twinge. Cool scents lulled him in his tracks and he stopped, forgetting the nectar and the comfort of his favorite chair. Yes, he thought, the angels! And entered the brink of stairwell with only the most minor of trepidations.

By the time he had wiped the dust from each of the many casks, he found that he was in somewhat more of a hurry than usual, more anxious, eager to see if the platinum locks would move, something maybe glance his way; an angel possibly tossing a smile, warm and safe beneath the glass. So he placed his arms around the polished breadth of stone and heaved, lifting the base onto its edge. But the angels refused to cooperate; insisting, like a kettle of drowned rats, on gazing inviolate into the depths. The man began to shake the cask with greater and greater abandon, using his dainty knee as leverage. Until suddenly, within the murky grunge, he saw a flutter, the slightest tremble of coagulated wing. Then, there! . . . the amber glint of terrestrial eye! And in his excitement he let go of the cask, the enormous weight crashing in a splintering explosion on the flagstones, liquid sweeping everywhere, a muck of angels glopped on the floor like chum from a pail.

And our man? The hero of our tale? He lay crumpled, a spear of onyx quivering in his groin.

But as to whether he thought of those angels, whether he remembered them as the light crawled from his brain, we don't know. We know only that when the staff returned, slightly more boisterous than usual and more than a little sunburned, what they found was found by smell and buried, warm tongues racing in the lull of a gossipy afternoon.

Index

Catherine Scherer

Garden of Eden. *See* Adam and Eve.
gestures, 46, 60, 77, 224.
  obscene, 36, 92, 112, 226, 281, 308, 359.
  symbolic, 309.
Gibralter, Rock of (allusion), 198, (illusion), 204.
goat, in aspic, 95, (recipe), 391-92.
  lecherous (epithet), 46, 82, 120, 150, 233, 234, 331.
  nude woman with, on bus, 162.
Gorgon's head, 377.
Greeley, Andrew. *See* author, Henry's accusations against, of
  agreeing with.
grunts. *See* self-defense, verbal.
Gunflint, Chert, 117.
Henry VIII, Henry's resemblance to, 97, 221, 265, 377.
Hermione, 119, 176, 184-86, 209, 245, 267, 318, 319, 320,357.
hooves, cloven, suspicions of, 99, 176-78, 319-20.
humdrum neurosis, 86-88, 157-59, 284-86, 382.
Icarus, 177.
impersonation, 336-47.
jawbone. *See* Heidelberg mandible.
jigsaw puzzle argument, 188.
Kriegfeld, Henry.
  age, first impressions, 8, 14; revised, 52, 196, 274, 381.
  bear skin auction, 221.
  British Army, service, 52, 196.
  coffee, iced, fondness for, near fatal, 342.
  first meetings, 4, 10-18, 34, 43.
  first verbal criticisms of author, 62, 92, 107.
  French kissing, first lessons, with author, 40, 62, 128.
   See also author, Irish experience.
  hobbies. See defloration, of virgins; erotica, card index of.
  jokes
   dogs, bitches; bitches in heat, 92, 175-76.
   finger in corpses's asshole, 318-19.
   Virgin Mary, 254-55, 367-68.
  legendary exploits, 67-69, 147-48, 253-54, 320-22.
  loss of youth felt, 188, 196, 377, 382, 390.
  nude, with musicians. *See* Lion House.
  nymphet period, 226, 235, 267.

visceral sensations, 13, 144, 214, 328, 398.
weapons, author's resort to. *See* women as warriors.
Worker's League. *See also* Labor League, parent org.; England.
    Alex and, 159-60, 163, 205.
    beauty parlors, after the revolution, debate, 202.
    capitalism, death of, 149-50, 183, 298.
    "last ideological gasp." *See* Segal, Erich, *Love Story.*
    Marx, (Heinrich) Karl.
        carbuncles, tactfully treated, 255.
        holiday at Margate. *See* sea-bathing, Marx and.
        "plagued as Job," 271-273.
        See also anecdotes, endearing, about Marx.
    revisionists, running-dog. *See* Sparticist League.
    "Trotsky." *See* baby's first word.

The Proofreader

Tim Hensley

"The stock is smashed repeatedly by type and travels along a back conveyor belt under heating ducts which bake the inc dry. An employee inspects the product and discards imperfections. The rest fall into a cardboard box and are then placed in a different cardboard box," the overweight woman siad.

She took a look at his application and offered him a rope of black licorice form a plastic tub on her desk. He was applying for the position of proofreader of wedding invitations. He wanted a part-time job while he went to school.

"Your previous experince was as a boxboy at Alpha Beta?" the overwight woman asked.

For the interview Brian wore a shirt with buttons and smiled but could not stop himself from noticing that the womans strapless top was too tight and it looked as if she had four breasts.

"Yeah. It was only a summer job, but I did become familiar with working around a conveyor belt," Brain replied.

He tugged at the rubbery strand as they talked.

The overweight woman adinistered a test in which he was to find as many mistakes as he could within a time limit. He passed.

The job secured, Brian weft the room and went into another room where the exit was. There he noticed a girl dressed in black typing at a computer terminal. Brian thought she was cute. She wore a red wristwatch, was tall and then, and had nostrils that looked like commas. Her fingers moved over the keys like a threatened spider. Brian wanted to speak to her but saw she was busy staring intently at what she was typing. He wished he was a sentence.

Brian got a parking ticket while being interviewed. The officer indicated his error with a blue pen.

Brian was nineteen years old and an english major at the local university. He found out about the proffreading job by looking on the schools job bored. He knew that when he received his degree, with his name on it, mechanically reproduced by a factory much like the one he was now employed at, he would have a true sign of his knowledge, and that then he could go out into the real world and find a real job.

In Brians room the carpeting had not been replaced since he was a child. It had a repeating pattern of squares, each filled with a cartoon character. These characters werre suffocated by a bed, crushed by a desk, and impaled by chair legs. When Brian entered he stepped on Mary Worths head. That night he dreamed he was inthe carpet. He could not leave it, only crawl into different boxes.

Brian was single and his many attempts at finding a girlfriend had failed. After waking up, he thouhgt of a solution to this problem. He decided that couples employ each other and that meeting someone was like a job interview. He decided not to wear his eyeglasses or flared pants. Perhaps he could echo yesterdays success! With the girl in black! He would try to make a good impression and would lie about his experience.

He turned on his TV. A beautiful woman was inside. She was on a game show called "Wheel of Fortune." She stood neXt to a row of boxes and when they lit up she spun them to reveal letters. These eventually formed a sentence. Contestants won prizes if they could guess the sentece before it was formed.

Signet Thermography was located on a street of intdustrial buildings that ended in a cul-de-sac. Each building on the street was required by law to display a sympol of four different colored squares with numbers in them to indicated hazard levels. At Cignet, for instance, there was a machine which manufactured matchbooks imprinted with the names of couples that could burst into flames unless carefully attended.

On his first day at work, Brian was given a rubber stamp with the letter "R" on it and a blue pen.

"The work comes in batches pinched by clothes pins. You indicate all errors with the blue pen using a system of symbols. Then you stamp this box on the customers copy with the "R" to show that you have read it," L said.

There were two other proofreaders at Signet and they also had rubber stamps with characters on them: L and B. L was an overwight man. When he walked his thighs rubbed together making a zipper sound. He spent most of the da$ exhanging gossip with B about wich employee was sleeping with which. B's love of gossip was driven by a fear that she might be in it. She smoked cigarettes and the matches that lit them came from the matchbook machines badly printed couples. Both L and B were married.

During the coffee break, L said to R, "So Brian, I bet you're a real stud with the ladies, eh?"

"Frank, you're terrible! Don't tease him," said B.

"You think i'm terrible?"

"You got it, honey."

"Well give me some penicillin so I can get rid of it."

"Ha-ha. What a card. We need to get rid of you."

Then B asked R if he had a girlfriend.

"Uh-uh."

"Well, you're young. I'm sure there are lots of girls just dying for a handsome young man like you."

"Uh, thanks. Who's that girl in black?"

"Ah Brian," said L, "think she's a hot number, huh? Her names Alison, she's a typesetter."

After break, the proofreaders resumed stamping with a three letter alphabet from which no words were formed.

R inspected hundreds of people deeply in love looking for errors. He, himself, was not allowed to make errors. He read in elegant script:

In this world of uncertainty and confusion, we too have found each other.

We request the honour of your presents.

We will be untied on June thirteenth.

At two o'clock noon.

The marriage will be consummated in the old house in memory of our deceased father.

Reception in rear of Our Lady of Sacred Heat.

R glanced at each word. Each word went through his eyes. Then each word traveled along a conveyor belt into a cardboard box. After a few hours, the words could only be understood as a string of letters in the correct order. His eyes began to water from hunching under the flourescent lamp above his desk.

"Sunlight isn't blue and doesn't flicker, while flourescemt light is and does," the optometrist later explained. "This causes eyestrain. Thsi eyestrain can be stopped by having your glasses tinted pink, Brian."

At the end of one of the batches, R found a note that read:

Dearest,

If you saw, say, a mailbox or a clothesline while walking down the street you would read it as if it were an invitation. But what is the grammar that forms the thoughts that describe the malebox, clothesline? I must see you. And you will proofread this invitation. But it's really in a foreign language. When you look at my face you will see acme or a beautiful nose. How? I am in love with you. Pleawe meet me in the bar of the fast lanes bowling alley at eight tonight.

Your secret admirrer

R did not completely understand the note but was excited. He capped his pen. He thought of Alisons lips covered with red ink, each kiss a reproduction of her lips.

R took a time card pith "Gerber, Brian" typed on it and placed it inside a slot where it was perforated.

As Brian left work, a couple entered the House of CArds StaionEry Shop and chose an invitation from Signet's "Momento Mary" line. Couples used Signet Thermograp, a company with over 200 employees, to create an image or object using language. This became a sign of their love.

By having his face phtographed and laminated, Brian became twenty-one.

Then he went to Sears to buy a blazer for his date. He stood on a conveyor belt which took him up to the Mens clothes department. He tried on coats in front of a mirror which split him into three. Each coat was not a coat but a lifestyle of coat wearing. Each Brian appraised himself and looked for faults. None of the coats fit trian that well. He bought one and the sales clerk desensitized it so it would not set off an alarm.

On his way out, Brian passed a line of toy children that came with birth certificates.

Patrons of the fast lanes bowling alley stepped on a rubber carpet to come inside.

At 8:04 Brian entered the bar. He toook a slow look around. It was dark. There was a jukebox and a row of stools. The jukebox played a love song that was interrupted by strikes. AFter he had made sure that Alison was not there he sat next to Foy, the overweight woman who had interviewe∂ him.

"Hello Brian, aren't you a little young to be in here?" she asked. She wore a black drss and bowling shoes. Brian noticed that her eyebrows and eyelashes were not real.
    "Well, I'm . . ."
    He began to feel hot in his coat.
    ". . . Listen Foy, i'm a little confused. Did you send me a note to meet you here?"
    She looked at the ice cubes in her glass.
    "You better kepp this a secret. I'm married. If you tell anyone I'll fire yoiu. That note was meant for Frank. I forgot it was in a batch of work you might see."
    Brian looked at his right foot.
    "Oh, I won't tell, cross my heart."

Brians shoes were put into a compartment. Then he wsa given

different shoes with numbers on them. He was also given a score sheet with a row of squares on it. In each square was a smaller square.

10 thrust his fingers and thub into the sockets and orifice of a bowling ball. He rolled the ball toward the pins. Kluunk! It came back on a conveyor belt.

The next day at work R learned that Alison had been fired. He sat at his desk and stamped. His spinal cord began to slouch into a question mark.

[Editor's note: When this story first ran, a number of readers failed to appreciate the obvious typographical subtext, ironically remarking on the "irony of such bad proofreading of a story entitled 'Proofreader.'"]

Flying Lessons

Michael Cole

In the alley behind the theatre, the textbook admonishes his neurotic roomate, "An entire audience of school buses, and you forget. Next time we do the helmet routine, hide the skull."

From its deep pocket, the mirror pulls an old photograph of clouds in a tree and shows it to the sparrow. "You see, I also taught your ancestors to fly."

This isn't embellishment, it's pain!" the stone cries. Another petrified tear hits the sculptor's floor.

Settlement cracks running from both walls, the ceiling gets up, takes a leak, then returns. "If you would hear me, listen to nuance." The baby grand doesn't understand.

"At my death, this song flies to your sleeping ears." The crippled sparrow is swallowed by a snake. The little girl rolls over in her sleep.

3 Word Stories
Richard Kostelanetz

Aren't you coming?

Boy meets girl.

My relatives died.

Is God generous?

She masticated rubber.

He became friendlier.

But we did.

Did you steal?

To withstand terror.

As it were.

She loves him.

Never had friends.

SHE BEGAT ANIMALS.

Lessen your vulnerability.

Don't fuck me.

He saw God.

Be aware now.

She became crazy.

In our beginnings.

Allow gross violations.

Don't you see?

HIS HEART FAILED.

She had excuses.

Wasn't it fun?

First   second   third.

She fucked her.

Credit your ancestors.

Wandering through darkness.

Shortest stories suggest.

Reality And Reality

Alfred Schwaid

Taxidermy is a nobler art than mummification, but outside of the movies has never been practiced on humans. It involves a relationship more intimate than cannibalism and we shy away from it.

"Do you remember the story, 'The Most Dangerous Game,' I think it was called, in which human beings are hunted for sport?"

"I most certainly do. It was also a movie but I don't remember which was better."

Shrinking human heads is a form of taxidermy, so maybe I'm wrong after all. But then again, head shrinking involves a more or less gross distortion of the object and taxidermy aims at verisimilitude so maybe the two are not alike.

"In that story doesn't he mount the heads of his victims and hang them on the wall as trophies?"

"Yes. That's why I mention it."

It was the sight of that moose head above the fireplace that caused me to bring this up. Who knows how long he had been dead? While the rest of him had mouldered away to a loamy substance his head was still intact and could be defined.

"What movie was it that ends with Bella Lugosi skinning Boris Karloff alive in preparation of mounting him?"

"That movie was more properly concerned with necrophilia, but human taxidermy was prominently involved so maybe there's a connection."

There is a connection between headhunting and cannibalism involving a belief in the soul and the transmission of spiritual qualities.

"A physical transmission of spiritual qualities."

"So you think it's a crude belief?"

"Can anyone tell us who killed that moose?"

"I can. It was Joe Polis. And he did it long before any of us were alive."

"There, you see? There's an interesting story involved with its death that would have been lost to us had its head not been preserved."

In that movie Boris Karloff kept the mounted body of Bella Lugosi's wife in his bed.

Would it be so terrible to visit the deceased in their lifelike forms and attitudes instead of talking to their graves?

This was once great country for moose hunting. Thoreau, present at the shooting of a lactating moose was repelled by the sight of mingled blood and milk. We have photographs now of blood mixed with milk. Cannibalism has not been particularly frowned upon when survival was at stake, unless it involved murder.

"Tomorrow I'll take you both out and show you some live moose."

When skinning out a moose's head the last thing to be detached is the nose.

"How do you feel about that? Do you think there are circumstances where cannibalism can be justified?"

"It's easy enough to sit here by a warm fire after a hearty meal and muse about the morality of cannibalism, but only think of the Donner party and you'll see that the question doesn't exist."

A taxidermist cannot flatter his subject. He's got to fit the skin as he has it. Can you think of another art where the model and the finished product are the same?

"You've already mentioned mummification. I might suggest music as another but the explanation would be too intricate."

Joe Polis was also a great canoe maker, I think. The fireplace was enormous, meant to heat a great hall, which this room resembled. It was made out of native stone of a type that was plentiful in that area. No need to transport them great distances, they were lying around for the taking. There were canoe birches nearby too, and I itched to peel the bark from one and try my hand at canoe making.

"His were as good as they come, but nowadays we use aluminum canoes."

Charles Rungius knew a thing or two about moose. He painted and sculpted them with a remarkable degree of veracity. He found them throughout Maine, Montana, Alaska and British Columbia. He would paint his sketches in the woods, of an animal that could be either majestic or ridiculous.

"Had you come in the winter I would have shown you the art of hunting moose on snowshoes."

I kneeled in the canoe behind him and watched his paddle thrust into the water's reflection, dispersing the clouds that were there, parting them as if they were curtains, my own paddle probing in unison. The mist had just recently lifted and I scarcely realized our motion: the lake seemed endless and we floating as delicately as a leaf. Had I not been concentrating on his paddle I could have been convinced we were drifting. Our arms were motivated by one system, commanded it seemed by neither of us, and even though we had not been paddling long I was lulled close to the borderline of stupor. Last night he told me the lake was bottomless. It would take forever to fall through it. Nothing had ever yet achieved it. Its surface that day was docile but I've since known it to be as capricious as mercury. He had crossed it many times without incident but I was uneasy because I couldn't swim.

The idea of bottomless lakes is prevalent, and persistent even though every one can be sounded. Our senses find it hard going against such a charged belief.

A theory has recently been developed that the Aztec nobility practiced cannibalism for the protein it provided. The practice of eating human brains in New Guinea leads to the transmission of a deadly disease.

We came to this place for its rusticity, one of the old hunting camps of the Maine woods.

"There are more moose here now than there ever were."

The old-timers might be right about that.

"They'll come right into your backyard in some places."

Which proves what a nuisance they've become. I have never seen a moose in a zoo but there are some fine ones mounted in the American Museum of Natural History.

If there are no known instances of human taxidermy, human skin has been preserved for various uses: among other things, razor strops, tobacco pouches and lampshades. Strips of the thigh are particularly good for razor strops, the breast and scrotum for pouches.

"I had heard of a book bound in human skin and I wanted to see it. Its contents were unimportant to me and I intended to leave them unimaginable but I wanted to touch the binding. Its owner was surprised that I had heard of it and was wary of my intentions. 'It's quite old,' he told me. 'The skin was obtained from a medical student . . . from an unknown cadaver.' I assured him I had no interest in exposing any secrets no matter what the case of its origin might be, that I intended to deal with it from the position of a spectator. 'It contains a collection of letters of no possible interest anymore to anyone. I haven't looked at it myself for ages. If you cherish rare bindings, this one, except of course for the material, is quite ordinary; if it had any value I would have sold it a long time ago.' 'Might I see it?' 'If you really want to,' . . . and he handed me a volume bound in a material of inflexible purity that I almost dared not touch. I held another's skin in my hand. 'You imagine another presence when you touch it but it's easy to romanticize.' This was altogether different from seeing a photograph or a grave; even the corpse in front of me would not have been as immediate as this momento of the semblance of reality. 'It has lasted a long time.'"

Joe Polis was an expert at calling moose using a rolled up cone of birch bark and he would have taught me had we met. The sound that he emitted was an irresistible lure that made a mockery of every instinct.

"If two friends are alone and starving one must eat the other."

"Why?"

"Who would prevent it?"

"Suppose they both choose to die."

"Who would allow it?"

The hunter had his choice of every cut of meat and generally ate the tongue first. Fresh meat roasted over a wood campfire is savory. The fire itself is reassuring. An ax is the most useful tool for dressing out a moose.

We came as close to the other side as we dared, holding the canoe out from the shore. An osprey announced us but Joe's call was too enticing and our quarry stepped out to have a look. We were downwind and safe from his perception. A massive rack of palmate antlers spiked with tines sat on his head like a molten halo, a surrealist's found candelabra. The osprey dove and broke the surface of the water to clutch for a fish. Nothing new yet for the moose to wonder at. I held us steady while Joe sighted in just behind the shoulder, fired, and his blood, loosed from its orderly conduits, spouted every which way inside of him.

I have on my desk an inkstand made of his hoof; an heirloom, in fact, from a day when one dipped one's pen in ink, and heard the scratching of a nib on paper. A taxidermist can mount the entire animal or make use of every part separately.

I had only a vague notion of that movie and a memory of two or three scenes but remembered that its theme was of betrayal. Two men were friends and one coveted the other's wife: pestilence, death and torture followed. It was made during a time when the actual skinning was omitted from the audience's view. I had to look into a copy of Vesalius to see a flayed human being. "The skin is an organ." Many popular accounts of skin care or pathology begin that way.

There was a railroad in those days too, and it carried you up along the river through a logged out area, with a spur into a little town that was the head of the logging operation. Hunters and fishermen took that spur and set out from there into the woods. Joe Polis had a backpack made out of juniper strips. If you were lacking anything in the way of supplies you obtained it there. I purchased a pair of suspenders. Joe advised me to buy some paraffin to waterproof our matches with. You melted the paraffin, inserted your matches into it and left them while it hardened: you had a block of solidified paraffin containing your matches which you need only break out one at a time as needed without ever worrying about whether they were going to be dry. You could immerse the whole without wetting a match. A short distance out of town you came to a burnt-out area where the ground and everything on it were completely black, including most of what was alive there: the only surviving moths and grasshoppers were black, the white and lighter colored ones, contrasting too greatly with their surroundings, having been eaten a long time ago. Snow, when it lay on that area looked like a type of mold.

"Joe lived over in Old Town but he was in the woods every chance he could get. He sold that head to my great-grandfather who claimed for as long as he lived that he had never seen a bigger rack."

I had seen one at least as big up north.

"They used to get them bigger than that up north."

"No more they don't. I used to think the same thing myself: there are moose bigger than that up north; but now I understand there aren't."

There's no reason there wouldn't be if they were there once.

The Masai used to drink a mixture of cow's blood and milk. They saw obvious nutritive benefits. A photograph had another purpose. When I saw it I could not, without the caption, have imagined what it was. It represented a form of suavity much different than that of Karloff and Lugosi.

The moose bogged down in deep snow becomes an easy prey for the hunter. The woods are dense and home to anything. The Masai graze their herds on open sun cleansed fields. Bright blood on white snow: burning bright, frozen blood or flowing into milk, one taints the other.

That fireplace might have been a good spot for Grendel's arm.

"Try to imagine it there."

"No telling now what it looked like."

A monster's arm.

"Assume it different from anything you've ever seen; concoct an original arm."

I have seen a taxidermist create a merman using the upper body and head of a monkey and the lower half of a fish. I have also seen a furred fish, another taxidermist's creation, a combination of fur and a trout. Dried skates can be carved and shaped into humanoid creatures. All of these things, as well as others, have been created to deceive us. Two-headed animals, though, have existed and have been favorites with taxidermists.

From Old Town we set out for the lake. It had been years since I had been there and I had long anticipated what we should find, burnished with years of memory, vivid with accumulated thought, a mental image but nonetheless real. Before this guide was born I had come here with his father and now I found while following him that they walked similarly. The woods were dark, as I remembered, and there were butterflies of a peculiar blue iridescence that I knew would be there. These were spared by birds because they were poisonous to eat. Moths and butterflies can be mounted but there is no need to call in a taxidermist for that.

"Actually there are several species and only one of them is poisonous. The birds can't tell the difference and leave them all alone."

"Your father told me that years ago."

"Yeah, he's the one taught me."

Looking at him and seeing his father as young as we were then

I understood that I had aged as we spoke.

"Nothing has changed, I hope, where we're going."

All of the intervening years during which he was born and his father had died and I had been away from here were in a deeper part of the woods.

"Probably hasn't very much."

Miles and years from here priests of Xipe Totec had dressed themselves in skins flayed from human beings. Because at the moment of its death the werewolf reverts to its human form it is impossible to obtain its pelt.

Although I had been here before, on my own I would have been as good as lost and I followed him as if I were a child. Light was disarrayed by the foliage and the eye was at a loss to distinguish, at times, one shape from another. Nothing easier than to get lost in the woods. Roger's Rangers had probably passed this way on their return from their raid on Saint Francis, and I remembered that one of them had managed to survive while others starved, by gnawing on a human head that he had managed to keep concealed in his knapsack.

The country was as pristine as you could wish. I looked for the trail his father had blazed but there was no longer any sign of it. The terrain became difficult and travel through it exhausting. I was bothered by flies and saw blood on my hands when I brushed them from my face. His face, I knew, was as bloodied as mine but he set it forward and continued at a rapid pace. Once or twice I must have fallen but scrambled to my feet and stayed close behind him: I irrationally imagined that if I failed to keep up he would have gone on without me.

"Pretty soon we'll come to where you'll see moose bigger than that one at the lodge. And no one else around here who knows a thing about it. I wouldn't guide anyone else in here for love or money."

It did not seem possible that an animal as bulky as a moose could penetrate this country but they moved around us with the alacrity of ghosts.

"They're going to the same place we are."

I remembered them years ago converging on the lake as if it were a sanctuary.

"The story is that it's where they originated."

Did he believe it?

"Why not?"

Though they were much thinned out in other places they remained there as plentiful as ever. The seasons cannot go backward but things there remained as they had always been.

Custer's horse was stuffed for display and the same can be done with pets. The origin of taxidermy is obscure. Did it derive pragmatically from attempts to decoy the living animal? An owl, or its image, is an effective decoy for crows.

The woods gathered darkness and condensed it. There was no longer any room for light. I plodded along behind my guide but began to feel his presence irksome. He wanted to reach the lake before nightfall but night and day were no longer relevant. The white disc that he consulted for direction could have been either the sun or the moon.

"He was a real guide, Joe was. Not like those around today."

"I brought my flute," he told me. "When we get there we'll have some music."

It seemed to me that we had already gone further then we should have. I would have thought that we had either passed the lake in the dark, or that it no longer existed. In an atmosphere as compact as that there seemed no possibility of a lake at all. The foliage flattened, became planar, and I followed him through it as if through a tapestry. A Steller's jay screeched around our heads with erratic persistence—its flight as frazzled as a moth's, and he seemed to want to pay attention to its voice. Objects should contrast with the spaces around them. He pushed ahead and I lost sight of him: he became as dark as his surroundings.

"He always wore a sash in the woods striped with bright colors."

I was as good as alone until I should approach him again. In the morning mist, whiter than milk, always rose from the lake, trees white as chalk. He stood gracefully posed and dark, a bird more suited to the south near him, and I heard the flute.

The Shrinking City

Lawrence Fixel

It is time to acknowledge openly what has already been verified by a number of independent sources: *our city is shrinking!* And this in spite of all efforts, especially in the past year, to further various "expansion" programs. These include raising the permissible height for new structures, as well as extending the city limits . . . . As for the reaction of our citizens, it is varied. Some still insist nothing has changed. Confronted with the evidence, they claim that it is our perception that has somehow been altered. Some have even suggested a temporary "affliction"—to be corrected by the compulsory wearing of special "magnifying" glasses.

All this brings us to a difficult point: is the same thing happening to us, the inhabitants? I refer now to my own experience: earlier this year I had already noticed the smaller size of the house, the furniture. One day, returning from work, I had to squeeze through the door. The next day, to my surprise, I was able to enter without difficulty. I decided to check my appearance in the full-length mirror in our bedroom: *There was no change!* It was only later that it occurred to me: but, of course, the mirror itself was now reduced . . . . This morning, on my way downtown, I recalled the old saying: "Never a disaster, but someone benefits." Yet as I thought of it, who could that possibly be? An obscure item in the morning paper caught my attention: model makers, toy stores selling miniature houses, doll furniture, report that business has never been better . . . .

1980

The Devil Trap

Thomas E. Kennedy

> *. . . and then she told a story about a boy*
> *who had the devil's heart in his hand and*
> *could kill him . . .*
>
> —Gladys Swan, *Gate of Ivory, Gate of Horn*

A boy and a priest were walking in the forest, looking for blackberries which they could sell in town for money to have the church door repaired. The boy was only a lad of seven, but the priest had let him come because he believed in the power of innocence against the darkness of the forest. As they picked their steps across a ragged field of briars, the sounds of a creature in agony came to them from the pine forest at the edge of the briar field.

They paused, listened. A moan of deep pain drifted across the summer air. In the silence that followed, a bird shivered, whistled. A fly sawed. The moan came forth again.

The boy said, "Something is hurt."

"It is not a good thing," said the priest. "I can feel it. Come, let's go away from here." But he saw the pure empathy on the boy's drooping lips, in his large light eyes, and was ashamed. What if he were mistaken? What if he were urging an innocent child to turn away from his own natural goodness, his own natural urge to give aid to a fellow creature in pain?

"Well, we can look then," said the priest. "Only look."

They changed direction, stepping through the brambles toward the pine wood. The air beneath the tall pines was dim, still. A thick carpet of brown needles cushioned their steps. When they had gone a little way into the wood, the moan again caught their ears.

"Over there," said the priest and led the boy around a thick cluster of dying saplings.

The moan grew louder, nearer. They turned past the last wall of the trees and stood before a very tall man hanging by his feet from a supple young pine. He writhed there and moaned and black blood dripped slowly from his mouth into a puddle on the earth beneath his head. At the center of the puddle lay a black, sleek, wet thing, pulsing and twitching.

"My God," said the priest. "My God, I've heard of this."

The hanging man looked at the boy, opened his lips. "Help me," he croaked. The man was naked and patched all over with black hairs. His eyes were black and gleamed with his agony.

The priest stepped forward cautiously to peer at the puddle of blood.

"He's lost his heart. It is the devil, lad, and his heart is fallen out of his mouth. It is a devil trap. I've heard of this."

"What can we do?" asked the boy, staring transfixed, into the gleaming pain of the hanging creature's eyes.

"This is a great good fortune for all the world," said the priest. He pointed at the boy. "You must take his heart in your hand and squeeze it to death. Then we all at last shall be free of him and his evils. Free at last!"

The boy looked into the eyes and did not move.

"Do it now, boy, quickly," said the priest. "Only an innocent can touch that black heart. If I put just one finger to it, my arm will be burnt to lava. Do it. Take it, now!"

The boy knelt beside the puddle, reached in and took the heart in his palm. It was cold as snow, but twitched and writhed there like some legless, faceless animal, drooling black ooze through his fingers.

"No," the devil whispered, moaned, "Please, boy. Mercy on me. I am old, sick. I have lived longer than the world and I am sad as only a very old man can be. I have never known such pain as this I experience now, this pain of death. It has taught me. I will change. Only put the heart back in my mouth. I will become good again, as I was those days before I turned against the Lord. I will kneel before him. I will beg his forgiveness. I will serve my Lord again."

"Do not listen to him," growled the priest. "He lies. Squeeze it. Kill him. Do it at *once!*"

The boy's fingers curled round the heart. He began to squeeze it in his fist. A tear rolled off the devil's eye, hung on his eyebrow, dripped to the earth. The boy squeezed harder. The devil groaned, twitched, wept. "Please, boy," he whispered, "I do not want to die. I will change."

"Do not listen," said the priest.

"Think of your poor mother," the devil said. The boy paused.

"Do not listen," said the priest. "He lies. He is all falsehood."

"Think, boy, if there were no mercy left in this world and your poor mother's heart was in the hand of a merciless child. Will you kill mercy, too?"

"He lies! You will not kill mercy! You will only kill evil!"

The boy looked from the priest to the weeping, pleading creature hanging in the tree. The devil sighed, the gleaming pain of his eyes began to film over to dullness. He said with great sadness, "The priest is right. What do I deserve? I have spent half an eternity fueling the evil in the hearts of others. Turning man against man. Nation against nation. Inspiring the vilest acts. Why, then, should you show me mercy?" The dying eyes looked up into the boy's face, the priest's face. "Forgive me," he pleaded, "so that, if God has more mercy than this child, I might at least rest in peace when I am dead."

The boy looked to the priest. The priest only stood there, mouth open, staring. The boy stepped forward. The devil's tongue lolled out of his mouth. The boy reached forward with the black heart. The devil's tongue shot forth like a viper's, curled round the heart, snapped it into his mouth.

Boy and priest stood, mesmerized, watching the devil swallow his heart. The process was long, strenuous. Perspiration shone on the devil's face. When at last the heart was in place again, the devil's body writhed, began to double up. He bent like a folded knife, his face gazing upon the stout rope round his ankles which attached him to the tree. He reached to the rope with his fingers, snapped it like a string, dropped to his haunches on the earth, and crouched there for a moment, gazing upon boy and priest with red eyes.

Then he rose to his feet and seized the priest by the throat, watched the man's agony as he squeezed life from him. The priest's eyes and tongue bulged, his face turned blue, the slightest of sounds creaked from his throat. Then his body went limp. The devil flung the lifeless husk from him, turned upon the boy.

The boy looked up into the face of the terrible creature. Slowly, a grin spread across the devil's face. He winked. Then spun and crashed off, running, through the forest.

Oh How Time Flies

Glenn Russell

A girl wearing a ruffled pink dress and sneakers hops on a merry-go-round and mounts what she thinks is a horse but is actually a sewing machine. She stretches her legs until her toes barely touch the throat plate. Perplexed, sensing something woefully wrong, she peers down at all the dials: tension dial, buttonhole dial, stitch-width dial, stitch-control dial, stitch-pattern dial, reverse-stitch dial. A bell rings and the merry-go-round goes round, lights flashing, organ music playing, horses and needle bobbing. Round and round she goes until her hands and legs swell with veins, her face puckers with wrinkles, and all her hair turns silvery gray.

The Feeder

Eve Ensler

When the cake arrived at his fourth birthday party it occurred to him right there, that this cake would never be enough, that no cake would ever be enough and he wept uncontrollably for three hours. Maybe it was the memory of this. Maybe it was because his father had literally evaporated in front of him. Whatever it was, he had become a feeder. He fed. He dreamed of feeding. It wasn't so much an obsession, as a way of life. He loved to watch people eat and he loved to be full. He loved thinking of the hungry no longer wanting. He imagined round and full stomachs, like babies, all quieted and asleep. He was not a fat man and he did not like obesity. That was something different. He did not use food. He did not like it because it covered up feelings or avoided the truth. He liked that it broke down in the digestive track. He could see it racing to all the needy parts of the body, the blood and the bones and the muscles and cells. He liked that the waste took care of itself and left when it was ready. He liked helping it leave.

At puberty the feeding fantasies began. He would envision skinny young girls. They would come to him starved, their rib cages exposed. He would help them. He would set a magnificent table. He would fill it with every food imaginable; turkeys and hams and potatoes and peas and breads and fruits and corn on the cob. He would sit the girl down at the head of the table. In front of her he would place a huge silver platter which he would fill with food. Then he would command her to eat. As she filled her mouth, he would place one hand on her stomach and the other on his cock. He would stroke himself as her stomach expanded. Only when the platter was emptied would he allow himself to come, which he did under the table. There were many variations of this fantasy, but always his orgasm came when the person was full. He married three women. Each of them had anorexia nervosa. The first two were incurable, but the third had become round. Now she loved to eat too. They lived in a small town and they owned a fast food diner. Needless to say, he cooked. He was very happy in his work. He stood behind a grill where he could watch the customers come in. They did not have menus in his diner. The customers did not order. He would watch them and then he would decide what they needed. He would not ask. He would just cook and then, his wife would serve. The people were always surprised, but then they were grateful. He seemed to have a perfect knack for knowing what they wanted. And, it was always delicious. For relaxation he would often go to the "Stop and Shop" which was open 24 hours a day. He would get a huge cart and slowly walk through the 27 aisles, filling up as he went. He loved to watch the families, their carts overflowing. He would pretend to be a child, going home with one of them. He would unload each item, savoring it as he put it in its place. He would fill the cabinets. There would be at least three boxes of everything and always enough milk. He *was* obsessed with that. He could not sleep at night if the refrigerator did not have at least two cartons of milk. This had been true since he left home. This habit drove the third wife crazy. She did not understand why they needed to have so much milk when neither of them drank it except in their coffee. It always went bad. And although she had come to love eating, she still hated an abundance of anything. She could only tolerate small amounts. Like when they ate ravioli, he filled his plate to the brim and she could only eat 8 at a time with a very limited amount of sauce.

When the third wife got pregnant, the man was wild with joy. She was hungry all the time and he loved going to get things for her. She never even needed to tell him what she wanted. He always knew. For the first time, she was undeniably full. She was growing. And there was another life, another hungry life, waiting inside. At night when she slept, he would rest his hand on her stomach and sometimes, without thinking, he would come. He was ecstatic. He loved her milky breasts and dreamed of them. Then one night the third wife went to the hospital. She bled for three days. When it was over, the baby was gone. The third wife was empty and flat. She had no appetite. The man stayed with her, but his pain was great. He lay down on the floor with his head between his hands and he wept uncontrollably. He did not think he would ever cry enough. He blamed himself. His sperm were not hearty. He had not eaten well.

When she was well again, he tried to make love to her. But each time he would imagine his feeble sperm, struggling listlessly, unable to reach her eggs. He would go limp. She told him not to worry, to forget about the baby for awhile. But it only got worse. He began to get thin. Food turned on him. He couldn't bear the sight of it. His wife, depressed at her husband's condition, regressed. She lost thirty pounds in the first two weeks. They closed the diner. Regulars would come and ring the bell, but no one would answer. People in the town began to worry. A friend had dropped in to visit and reported that he was sure that both of them would soon evaporate. Somewhere in the third week, the husband and wife began to lose consciousness. They started to have visions, mystical and strange. They no longer felt irritable or depressed or even impotent. They hallucinated monkeys and zebras and umbrellas that floated around the house. They spoke to dead relatives on the phone. They saw themselves old and senile and they saw themselves die. They saw brilliant colors and they heard music, celestial music with a strange primitive beat. When they were found, they were crawling around on the floor as if in a nursery. They spoke to each other in baby language, "goo goo, goo ga," and they seemed to understand.

In the hospital they were fed intraveneously. A wonderful pink color returned to their cheeks. In a few days, their minds returned as well. The sugar-water made the man very hungry. He tried to resist, but the sight of his wife's thinness was more than he could stand. He ordered out for both of them. He ordered fresh salad and bread and pasta with marianara sauce. He ordered chocolate cake and ice cream. When it arrived, they ate. They ate solid for one week. They did not speak, but to order. They just chewed and swallowed and occasionally smiled at one another. They became round again. They left the hospital and reopened the diner. People in the town celebrated. They baked a cake the size of a drum. When the man saw it, he laughed. He knew he could make a baby. He knew there was enough of him to go around.

Baby's Head

Lee Nelson

"This world's no place for kids," Pam said. "The air's poison, the water's poison, the trees are all dead. A baby could strangle itself or fall on its head or eat lead paint. And even if it survives, it'll just die in a nuclear war, or face famine and disease and all that. I'd rather get run over by a truck," she said. "Or eaten by a shark."

Pam lived with her husband, Martin, and together they earned enough to pay for their diversions: the opera, the theater, the Philharmonic, the ballet, mountain bungalows, horse-back riding, ski trips, boat trips, big dinners after which they'd smooth their stomachs and sigh: "No place for kids. No place at all." Relatives, however, felt otherwise, or at least acted that way, winding up with infants: nieces, nephews, cousins. It wasn't long before Pam was put upon to babysit.

"Baby, baby, baby, baby." Pam's sister, Jill, was saying goodbye to six month old Robby. "Be a good baby, baby, baby, Robby-Bobby." Words didn't matter; sounds, smiles, facial contortions proved sufficient. Robby drooled and reached up with hands and feet. Pam sat on the sofa, kneading her fingers. "I'll be back in an hour or so," Jill said to her. "He'll take a nap in a little while." She bent close to Robby and screeched: "But maybe he's all excited! Maybe he's all excited! All excited! All excited! All excited!" Robby practically choked on his ecstasy.

He settled down as soon as Jill left. From the sofa Pam could see his hands playing with a string of colorful disks suspended across the carriage. Pam stood up and looked in at the pink head: a doll's head but with blue, glistening eyes not fixed on this or that, just watching the air, just glowing there too big for their sockets. "What's he thinking?" Pam asked out loud. "What's in his brain?" Some friends claimed to remember themselves as babies. For Pam that was hard to imagine. She remembered herself as a little girl but never as a baby. She couldn't imagine existing as a baby. "He's not thinking anything," she concluded and sat back down. Sometimes she thought that her memories of girlhood arose because she still felt like a child, that once she became an adult she would acquire an entirely new set of memories. Martin, who was clearly an adult, had predicted that Pam would mature sooner or later; it was inescapable: a stage of life, not a decison. "And a person doesn't need to have offspring in order to lead a full life," he had emphasized. "In some cases, we show more wisdom by remaining childless." Pam had agreed. But now she caught her breath and wrestled with her fingers and felt maturity at least an hour away. Until Jill returned, Pam had to keep her eyes on little Robby.

"Oh, please go to sleep. Please go to sleep."

She approached the carriage. Robby lay wide awake, eyes bright, hands grasping. She reached down and took him by the ribcage. He was soft and solid. He shaped his wet mouth into a triangle and gurgled. Pam stirred him just a bit, and he laughed some more. "Good baby," she said. "Be a good baby." His heavy head lolled back, then forward; the eyes sparkled for an instant; then without warning he lunged for the side of the carriage and froze, staring at the pine-wood floor, stunned as if surveying the world for the first time.

"Hard, shiny floor," Pam said in her natural voice. Robby swayed there, still in Pam's grip, his mouth open. "Hard, pinewood floor."

Robby squirmed like a turtle, thrusting out as far as he could. Pam studied the wispy hairs on the back of his head. Like a raw egg, she thought. Robby's hands hung down and slapped the side of the carriage, reaching for the wheel.

"Why do you want the wheel?" Pam asked, trying to sound pleasant. "You'll just get your little fingers caught in the nasty spokes."

A fly buzzed by.

"Oh no. I hate flies."

It buzzed again and darted up. Pam went to lay the baby back, but he resisted.

"Let's go. Time for your nap."

The fly buzzed again.

"Time to lay back down. So I can kill the fly."

The fly circled, then landed at the base of Robby's head, where the skull joined the neck, touching down instantly motionless, as flies could do, as if incorporeal. It rested among the golden hairs for a second, and beneath the added weight the neck-bone snapped and the baby's head dropped off and thumped against the floor, like a ripe fruit—a grapefruit or a coconut—simply detaching from the neck and falling, bouncing once, then rolling under the sofa.

"Oh my God!"

Pam fell to her knees and looked. The head lay glinting near the wall, beyond her reach. She raced into the kitchen and came back with a broom and streching under swept the handle from left to right and knocked the head out, but knocked it too hard, for it sped along the wall and caromed into the kitchen, straight into the space between the refrigerator and the stove, the awkward space she never cleaned.

"Oh my God!"

There it stopped, face to the wall, wedged between the two appliances.

The doorbell rang. Pam couldn't pretend not to be home. She'd answer the door and come back and pry the head free; she'd use a plastic container to block the opening so it wouldn't carom elsewhere.

"Let's just hope it doesn't roll by itself!"

Through the peephole she spotted the mailman and opened up. He smelled sweaty and was squinting at the manifest.

"Does a 'Solomon Breakwater' live here?"

"No. He lives next door."

"There's nobody home next door."

Get rid of this person, Pam told herself; her knees were trembling.

"I have a package for a 'Mr. Solomon Breakwater.'"

"Yes. Yes."

"Okay if you sign for it?"

"Yes. Yes. Yes. Yes."

As he handed her the clipboard, the baby's head rolled between their feet and started down the stairs. Pam gasped. The mailman had seen the head and was expecting an explanation. His strong, grey eyes had fastened on her, had become deadly serious. "It rolls by itself!" was all she could blurt out.

By the time she reached the bottom step, the baby's head had bounded through the vestibule—the door was propped open by the mailman's cart—onto the sidewalk and under a parked car. Pam prayed it would catch beneath the muffler or bounce back toward the curb; instead she watched in horror as the head continued into the street, angling for the sewer. But before it reached the drain, a tractor-trailer with eighteen tires and a blazing, chromium grill roared by and ran over the head with every wheel on the driver's side.

Pam understood that the headless torso she returned was not the same as the complete baby. Still, it was the best she could do. Rubbing her hands, she explained what had happened and then withdrew as Martin tried consoling Jill, who rocked on the sofa. Martin had hurried home after learning of the accident and now sat with his arm around his sister-in-law, his studious, bearded face explaining how loss was part of life, randomness and accident measurements of Being; how they needed to grieve, then move on: the planet still revolved. Jill closed her eyes and shivered. Pam marveled at her husband's gentleness; she would never have found the right words. She thought of his weak eyesight, his near blindness without glasses. Tears came to her eyes as for the first time she remarked to herself how much Martin resembled her father.

Love Worms

Patricia Eakins

An excerpt from

The Marvelous Adventures of Pierre Baptiste
Father and Mother, First and Last
Including His Life, Times, Friends and
Baleful and Voluptuous Beasts

I'm going to tell the love worms now.
Tell and tell.
You know them, some of you too well.
Are those the worms that live in hair of the dogs that watch our
spotted and brindled cows?
Oh, call them that.
Are those the worms that slip into our milkmaids' hearts?
The women know this, all too well.
Then tell and tell.
They say these worms resemble the hairs of the dogs that herd your
sister's cows.
Whose sister's that?
That's mine, yes, so never mind.
Then tell.
But what is the color of these worms?
They're lying in my brown dog's hair?
Yes, yes.
They're lying in my black dog's hair?
Oh, yes.
You tell me, what color are those worms?
Those worms are white, friends, white, white, white. And so you
see, that young white dog, he's rubbing his tickles, rolling on his
back—don't you know why he groans and moans?

Oh pity him, itchy beast.
Speaking of pity, who's that coming?
Pity him, itchy miserable beast.
Somebody's sister?
Pity him.
She. Has. Been. Warned. Yet—
Pity him, poor sad beast.
She parts the hairs of the dog to find the fleas—
Oh no!
And worms glide beneath the nails of her fingers to rest in the moons.
Oh no!
So bright the moons of her nails!
Oh no!
She strokes and strokes the dog.
Oh no!
So bright the moons of her nails!
Oh no!
She strokes the dog, and strokes him, while more and more worms slip under her nails.
Oh no!
Sh-h-h-h. She is sleeping. She feels no pain, only restlessness, yes, a sigh disturbs her. She is sniffing the air. She would like to smell a man and does not care who.
Your sister?
No, your mother.
Your mother?
It must have been your mother's sister.
Old aunt? Even she?
Don't you see? It could have been anyone, sneaking around in the bush, breathing hard outside the walls of the houses near the sleeping places of men.
Was she after my brother?
Oh, yes.
After my husband?
What do you think?
Son?
He's old enough—just ask him.
Father?

He's not too old, nor is grandpa.
After the master?
You need to ask? She wraps her legs around this man, around the stranger, lurking here, her heart explodes.
What?
From the worms.
Oh sure.
Don't laugh. She's dead.
So soon?
She won't come back.
That's all?
Not quite. The worms are crawling from her nipples, bright white worms like living milk.
Oh milk of life!
Though she be dead, yet no one who is mourning or washing her body is able for long to keep from stooping to kiss her breasts, not even the watching dogs.
Milk indeed. So it's starting again?
Already you see it.
Why? Oh why?
Who has not asked? Who? But our men are wise. They squat on their heels around the dead one.
Kissing, even they?
Don't you see? They hold each other back.
And the women?
Don't you see that bent old crone?
You mean your wife?
I thought she was yours.
No, you're mistaken. It's your sweetheart.
I'll take that one—see how she straightens her back.
My! What breasts!
Knowing what she has to do has made her patient and wily; her importance has restored the strength to her spine.
Truly, it seems to be as you say.
See how she blackens the dead one's nipples with mud and dung?
How they shine! Dark shine!
Now the bodies of the worms glitter in the muck on the nipples.
We see.
Do you? More and more worms?

Yes, yes, yes.
Then flip those wormy mud crowns into the coco rinds of water!
Flip them now! Flip! And fall yourselves to the ground, writhing
in tangles like drowning worms. Do it, now, without delay.
Pity us.
I pray for you.
Pity us.
I ask the help you need.
Oh help!
And now—
Is help coming?
Now—
Help on the way?
Now—
Help?
Don't you see her, that old woman, walking without her cane, her
eyes quite clear, reading on the surface of the water in the coco rind
the names of the hapless sisters—
They! They!
Sneaking from their houses to the cow pens by the trees—
No!
To pet the dogs—
Oh no! No! No!
Didn't they do it?
No!
Are you sure?
Yes.
Confess!
*I am guilty. I. I have petted the dogs and loved the glow of the worms
in my nails.*
*I. I am as bad as you. I have petted the dogs and lusted after strange
men of other tribes who would steal our cows.*
Shall you die with the sister whose poor dead body is before us?
Let us live.
Let us live.
Let us live!
Enough. Already what you ask is done. Do you see the old one,
sewing the earrings of dried dead love worms into the living
women's earlobes?

Yes.
And see the sisters who wear the earrings digging the pit for the dead one?
Yes.
Though the sewing is painful—
The punishment is just.
You will endure?
We will endure without grimacing or whining, in silence.
The punishment is just.
But does the charm work?
In time. Over years. Only women who wear the earrings may lie with the husbands of others.
Stay away from that man, Sluts.
Only women who wear the earrings give birth to gods—
The gods are with us!
No sooner be a god conceived than the earrings do crumble to dust. The mother falls asleep; her belly swells.
And the god in the belly?
He is kicking his mother, who cries in her sleep, her belly bucking.
He is being born. Pull! Push! Pull! Push! Ah! Ah! Ah! Ah! Where is he?
You know the gods are born invisible, but larger than men, to walk into the forest on their airy legs. Do you know?
We know the gods, though we cannot see them. Oh gods! Hear us now. Do not go far! Oh gods! Eat these foods we set out before you, the best we have, fish and porridge, callaloo—all your favorites. Gods! Take care of us as we take care of you.
You are right to placate the gods. They are difficult persons, difficult from the moment of their difficult births.
Good gods!
Good.
Never say the gods are bad.
When the mother of a god awakens from her dream of birth, her belly is flat.
Of course.
But there is more.
How could there be?
Listen!
We listen.

When she awakens, with her belly flat, the dogs are gone from the shadows by the cow pens.

Gone? The cow dogs?

Why are you worried? The dogs were wormy.

They had lived among us a long time.

Never mind. The dogs return, one by one, padding from the darkness of the god's forest, their tails wagging, to sit again with our home fires' shining reflected in their eyes.

If we drive them away, the gods themselves will come.

They will poison the wells.

They will sicken the cattle.

They will kill the babies before they are born.

You know how it is. The dogs are needed to herd the cattle, givers of food and wealth, yes, givers of hide and horn, milk and meat.

You are with us, gods!

Do not fail!

You are with us.

Permit us to please you.

You are with us.

We thank you. We bear the honor of this life with pride.

We honor our dogs, we honor our cows, and we honor our women in love and birth.

There's A Lid To Fit Every Pot

Edouard Roditi

This morning I woke up alone, abandoned by my lid and already feeling widowed. Years ago, my mother once warned me that a lid can prove to be very flighty, so that I was not unduly surprised to find myself now abandoned by my legitimate partner, and I soon consoled myself by remembering that, in any well appointed kitchen, one can always meet at a pinch other lids which can temporarily serve as substitutes for the absentee, though they may not always fit as neatly or as snugly. Anyhow, this evening, I already found myself in partnership with a soup plate that managed to cover me adequately enough while I was being used to boil some carefully peeled potatoes.

Although I soon became quite friendly with this piece of household crockery which had been imposed on me as a partner, I was still wondering where my delinquent lid might well be, and I even began to feel some mild twinges of jealousy. But would my own lid likewise feel jealous if it now turned up to find me merrily simmering under a strange and improvised lid? Would my lid accuse me not only of adultery, but of some even worse crime, such as that of shamelessly cohabiting with a member of an entirely different species? Was I really committing, however unintentionally and certainly not by any choice of my own, some strange kind of bestiality or at least of miscegenation? Are there any laws of Apartheid that might apply in a kitchen? Even a pot has a conscience, and mine was beginning to trouble me.

Meanwhile my soup-plate partner and I were discovering that we had many ideas in common, especially in such matters as politics and ethics. Although it was no longer very handsome, but somewhat cracked and chipped, it had originally belonged to a rather good set of dishes of which it appeared to be the only survivor, and it could boast of bearing, on its upper side that was beyond my field of vision, a pattern which had at one time been considered representative of rather gracious living.

But would my delinquent lid now be as haunted as I by guilt-feelings, I mean about having abandoned me, or even by feelings of shame, should it at this very moment happen to be used, for instance, to cover a child's stinking chamber-pot, which is after all the punishment that I feel that it truly deserves? And how would I react, were my lid ever to return to me from this kind of degrading adultery?

Such thoughts were leading me to remember what my mother had repeatedly told me many years ago: that there's a lid to fit every pot, although she never added that there must also be a pot to fit every lid. With this last comforting thought in mind, I can settle down to face calmly a lidless future of possible promiscuity, ready to be content with whatsoever substitute or improvised lid turns up from time to time to cover me. For all I know, my own long-lost lid may even in the long run turn up again. But would we still recognize each other after each of us has found itself in temporary partnership with so may other lids or pots, so many of which any well be, like my rather friendly soup-plate of today, of a very different species? Be that as it may, it's clearly not in Heaven that lids are made to fit pots.

Equus Caballus

Eric Basso

A change of wind and the leaves are driven into random piles with a quiet rustling. They scatter, eddying out across the mountain slopes in long irregular drifts. The site we have named "Equus Caballus" lies, by common consent far below any fall of dead leaves, in a narrow ravine sunk away from the light, where basalt columns once cut a deep pass through the grassy dunes.

Peering up from the edge of the talus . . . Lichen-spotted rocks blot up the lower sky. A chill turns each breath into mist. At break of noon the winter sun hangs pale beyond the cliffs. The peaks of the horn cast a blue shadow over half the valley. Some of this is in the riddle retold by one of the wives. We have it on tape with the other statements. It gives me an odd feeling I can't explain, the sense of a hidden connection behind the words, behind pieces I might eventually be able to fit together, if I could find them or be sure that they exist at all.

Something has been deliberately withheld. I won't say that the old women have been lying. It's more likely that each of them has been given a highly selective quantity of information and that each remains in complete ignorance of what the others have experienced below ground. I have never seen them talk among themselves. And each claims to be the wife of the great horse.

I go over the material again, knowing full well that it was a mistake for us to have come this far in our wanderings beneath the earth-crust.

This quest for the great horse. I realize, now that it's too late, where all our efforts are leading, and yet I go on. Even if I really have been snatched from the crater depths (another puzzlepiece leading where but to the beginning, to a time when the ravine had no name; a search party could have found me lying in the tunnel with my eyes closed and might have carried me back to the tent without my having been aware of what had actually happened, of what had come before or even a long time after my fall), I remember only the tunnel wind, oceanic gusts out of a dream that make me wonder if in fact I am not still asleep or dying.

I lay my hand on the taboret one last time and cannot say for sure whether it is my hand or the hand of someone strange to me, since all feeling has gone out of it. Consider the evidence: a network of breathing pores, an intricate weft of crevices and flattened hairs ashine like gold threads in the lamplight; the veins, traces of eggshell-green beneath the skin, shot through with fibrous tinges of purple, run among the blotches and speckles of old age.

I feel a sudden wisp of air cut through by nonexistent fingers. A breeze of dust and cinders. Other fingers move against the dark.

Our first time down we passed faces sketched in water and crystal, small subterranean landscapes glimmering at every overhang. The surface is far from smooth; we wear gloves not only for the cold but as a shield against the tines of ice that hang, fringes of bristly needles, from each ledge.

We dug our crampons into the ravine wall. We went down. Our headlamps gleamed—stippled lightballs undulating in the crust of ice. Between the darkness and the gradually thickening mist you hardly know what to expect. Odd forms take wing before your eyes; when you stop to look after them, you become distracted. A sudden rain of icechips on your shoulders is more than enough to throw you off balance. All too often jagged pieces, chiseled from the icewall by the climber directly above, would knock at the crown of my helmet with a dull concussive thud that sets my teeth on edge now as I recall it, lying here on my back with the lamp burning out beside me on the wicker matting.

I haven't been able to turn up the wick. Let it go out. I can think more clearly in the dark. I may even try to move my lips or wiggle one of my fingers. Till then I've got my shadow—they should be able to see it from the other side, if anyone is still out there: a black recumbent figure, halfway up the drooping canvas, pullulates against the blood-red dying of the lamp. With the hoot of the owls to lull me, I imagine nocturnal eyes, pairs of disembodied coals aglow in the lower branches of the cedars. Amber-green to yellow, the jackals' eyes come to me from afar. I hear the snow jackals baying at the new moon, and I remember waking in the middle of the night to the overpowering stench of urine and bloodied animal hide. A living weight pressed in on me. I felt its heartbeat through the canvas. Its foul breath's heat grazed the shell of my ear. A jackal had stopped to scratch itself against the outside of my tent, inches below where my shadow hangs and makes itself one with the dark where I see, without yet being able to feel the cold mist as it rises on my face, the fragment of a basalt column, emerald-green in the ice, a vague lightpool close to my eyes for a while longer, a little while longer, while I wait to form the words on my lips. To be able to move them again . . . I lose my footing. After what seems like hours, I step down onto something that is more than a toehold in the slippery icewall. I dig my crampons in. The ground should be giving way beneath my feet. But it's solid, buried under a thick sheet of ice.

A step back. Then another, and my balance goes, pitching me forward. The icewall is a blur. I can't quite bring myself to let go of the hammers. As long as I stay in this awkward position—my boots embedded up to the heel in the icecrust—I feel a dull throbbing at my ankles. A stabbing pain shoots into the joints of my knees. The pain deadens. My legs feel as if they're about to snap. No circulation. A cold prickly wave creeps up the lower extremeties. Does he feel it too, the numbness, if he has been climbing down at this same rate, step by cautious step on the pitons I have driven into the wall? I'll be hearing the tinkle of boot-spikes a few feet above. Come a few feet more. The echo: sounds of an ax chipping splinters of ice through the mist.

Mist and the darkness cover everything. I might be fogbound, lost in the midst of open country, and still feel these vaporous paws cupping my ears, muffling what would, if I could hear them, be the last breaths of someone quite near. The geologist, come at last . . . My own breathing whispers its pulse of blood back on my eardrums, a high whine of never-absolute silence, mummified by shell-like suctions of air. It takes the hypothetical form of a wedge, invisible as it fills the middle space. The volume of the wedge is at best an approximation, but it no longer interests him; given his less than perfect means of calculation, the geologist has repeatedly claimed that it would be no more than a thirty or forty foot drop to the base of the ravine from the topmost ledge. Long past forty feet, with no rope to grasp in case of accident, the fear of falling makes me lose all track of time. I don't know how far we've come, but it seems to me that the distance into "Equus Caballus" has varied radically with each journey down. Evidence of this, and of many other less momentous inconsistencies, I am forced to keep to myself. Even if I could regain the power of speech, I would hesitate to bring the matter up. The "evidence" is no proof that there is something in the mist and ice. *Something in the mist and ice,* I had written as much on the board before my collapse. The engineer seems to have an inkling. He comes into my tent each night to feed me chicken broth. He gives me all the latest news, and while he talks I try to think my way through the icecrust. A change...

> a change, where mist thickens in the lower cli-
> mate; find a way to melt the ice and the mist
> evaporates of its own accord—the hitherto mea-
> sureless ravine might then be found to be nothing
> but a shallow trench.

Undoubtedly, the ravine exists.

FIRST ACCOUNT OF THE PRESENCE OF ICE IN SO UNSEEMLY A PLACE. GREAT CHUNKS OF IT BECOME DISLODGED FROM THE ICEWALL SEEMINGLY WITHOUT HAVING BEEN TOUCHED IN ANY WAY. THE SHEER WEIGHT OF ONE OF THESE PLUMMETING OBJECTS, BE IT A TERRACE, A SHINGLE, OR AN ENTIRE LEDGE, IS MORE THAN ENOUGH TO KILL A MAN OUTRIGHT AND SEND HIS BODY HURTLING THROUGH THE MIST.

THUS FAR WE HAVE BEEN LUCKY. NO MEMBER OF THE EXPEDITION INTO EQUUS CABALLUS HAS BEEN KILLED, BUT TOO MANY OF US HAVE NOTED THAT THE ICE CHUNKS FALL ONLY IN THE PATHS OF OUR CLIMBERS. IT IS ASSUMED THAT AT LEAST ONE OF THE MEN WOULD HAVE HEARD ECHOES OF FALLING DEBRIS FROM OTHER PARTS OF THE RAVINE, BUT THIS HAS NOT BEEN THE CASE.

WE ARE THEREFORE CONVINCED THAT THE ICEFALLS ARE DELIBERATE.

AS ENGINEER TO THE EXPEDITION I FEEL COMPELLED, FOR REASONS OF MY OWN, TO SET MY THEORY DOWN ON PAPER.

MY HYPOTHESIS RESTS ON THE SUPPOSITION THAT A SPE-CIAL INTELLIGENCE IS AT WORK BEHIND THE ICE. AT LEAST A PARTIAL CONFIRMATION OF THIS IS TO BE FOUND IN THE TESTIMONY OF THE THREE OLD WOMEN, WHICH HAS BEEN TAPED AND WILL BE ENTERED INTO THE RECORD AT THE APPROPRIATE TIME. WE MAY INFER FROM A STATEMENT MADE IN ONE OF THESE TAPES THAT THE

HORSE, FEARING THE PRESENCE OF INTRUDERS, CONSTRUCTED, OR CAUSED TO BE CONSTRUCTED, A MECHANISM WHICH WOULD GIVE HIM CONTROL OVER THE ONLY KNOWN ACCESS TO THE SITE EQUUS CABALLUS —THE RAVINE WALL. IT IS GENERALLY BELIEVED THAT THE BASALT COLUMNS WHICH MAKE UP THIS WALL TAKE THE NORMAL HEXAGONAL SHAPE (EVIDENCE OF A CENTURIES' OLD LAVA-FLOW / FURTHER CONFIRMATION: THE PRESENCE OF AN EX- TINCT VOLCANO AT THE VERY BOTTOM OF THE RAVINE).

1.) THE ICE IS FORMED BY THE AGENCY OF THE SAID MECHANISM WHICH CONSTITUES A POW- ERFUL ELECTRO-CHEMICAL OR HYDRAULIC GEN- ERATOR, CONNECTED BY MEANS OF A HYDRO- THERMAL ENGINE TO A SERIES OF TAPS OR UNDER- GROUND CONDUITS. THESE CONDUITS GIVE ON A COMPLEX OF IRRIGATION PIPES RUN UP THROUGH THE LITHOSPHERE, TERMINATING ALONG THE RAVINE WALL IN A MORE INTRICATE MAZE OF FLEXIBLE HAIR-THIN TUBES THAT ASSUME THE ROLE OF CAPILLARY NERVE-ENDINGS BENEATH THE "EPIDERMIS" OF THE BASALT.

2.) ACTION OF THE MECHANISM: WATER FROM A SUBTERRANEAN MINERAL SPRING, COOLED AT FIRST BY AN ARTIFICALLY INJECTED AIR-MASS, LOWERS ITS TEMPERATURE AS IT RISES BEHIND THE WALL AND PASSES MORE RAPIDLY THROUGH CONDUITS OF SMALLER AND SMALLER DIAMETER. THE WATER EMERGES FROM THE BA- SALT COLUMNS THROUGH BILLIONS OF MICRO- SCOPIC PORES AND FREEZES ALMOST AS SOON AS IT MAKES CONTACT WITH THE COLD SUNLESS AIR. (IT IS POSSIBLE THAT THE DRASTIC FALL OF TEM- PERATURE THAT ONE EXPERIENCES ON THE CLIMB DOWN IS ALSO ARTIFICIALLY MAINTAINED. THIS WOULD ACCOUNT FOR THE PRESENCE OF AN IM- PENETRABLE MIST UNDER SUCH UNWARRANTED ATMOSPHERIC CONDITIONS.) DURING THE COURSE OF THIS OPERATION THE HYDROTHERMAL ENGINE REMAINS AT REST.

3.) ALTERNATE ACTION: WHEN ACTI-
VATED, THE HYDROTHERMAL ENGINE, OPERAT-
ING AT LESS THAN HALF ITS REQUISITE POWER,
HAS THE CAPACITY TO HEAT 800 GALLONS OF
WATER TO THE BOILING-POINT IN LESS THAN 3
MINUTES.

4.) ANY INCREASE IN FLUID MASS IN-
CREASES THE VELOCITY OF THE WATER BY 4. WHEN
THE WATER HAS BEEN SUFFICIENTLY HEATED BY
THE HYDROTHERMAL ENGINE, THE HYDROSTATIC
EQUATION IS THEN APPLIED BY FIXING THE DIS-
TANCE FROM THE WATER-SOURCE TO THE SEC-
TION OF THE ICEWALL TO BE DISLODGED. THE
RESULTING DISTANCE IS THEN COORDINATED TO
THE QUANTITY OF LIQUID MASS PER CUBIC FOOT,
WHICH IS ITSELF DEPENDENT UPON THE DEGREE
OF PRESSURE REQUIRED TO DISLODGE A GIVEN
BLOCK OF ICE (WHOSE DIMENSIONS WILL VARY
ACCORDING TO WHIM).

5.) THE TIME FACTOR IS CRITICAL. HAVING
COMPLETED ALL THE NECESSARY CALCULATIONS
IT REMAINS A QUESTION OF CHANCE WHETHER
THE BOILING WATER, HAVING RUN ITS COURSE
FROM THE HYDROTHERMAL ENGINE TO THE "CAP-
ILLARY NERVE-ENDINGS" IN THE RAVINE WALL,
WILL HAVE CUT THROUGH THE BLOCK OF ICE IN
TIME FOR ITS DOWNWARD TRAJECTORY TO HAVE
ANY ACCURACY IN REFERENCE TO ITS MAIN OB-
JECTIVE, THE DOWNHILL CLIMBER WHO IS TO ALL
INTENTS AND PURPOSES A MOVING TARGET.

6.) THE ACTION OF THE FLEXIBLE "CAPIL-
LARIES" IS SYSTALTIC. THE RAPIDITY OF THEIR
HYDROVASCULAR CONTRACTIONS LENDS THE
WATER ITS SHARP NEEDLELIKE EFFECT UPON
EJECTION.

AS I HAVE ALREADY STATED, NO ONE HAS BEEN KILLED OR INJURED
BY THE FALLING ICE. THE REASONS FOR THE HORSE'S FAILURE IN
THIS RESPECT ARE ALL TOO OBVIOUS.

Of all the forms that take shape here in the dark, my own is the last I wish to return to. One step back, one last step onto thin air.

I watch, as I did then, with a curious sense of detachment. The moment of watching is prolonged out of all proportion to the split-second it takes for me to realize that I haven't touched bottom. I am going to fall . . .

My gloved hands slide soundlessly down the length of the icehammer handles. A hail of grapeshot pummels my helmet with a sudden deafening tattoo, jerking the visor down over my eyes. I cannot see the last contact my hands have with the hammers before the weight of my body carries me down . . .

It wasn't like that.

I was falling. The crater darkness came tunneling back toward me. A separate incident, nothing like the near-accident on the ice above.

The sensation of having fallen remains, without the mist. A gas flame quivers in the distance, lighting up the other end of the tunnel —concentric rings of a gradually darkening blue run from the nucleus to the farthest perimeter until there's nothing but black space between me and the dimmest of these reflections.

Once thing almost all the equestrian portraits have in common is that placid expression. In all but two of the earliest sketches the eyes are slightly veiled and seem to fix on you with a diffident yet peculiarly hypnotic stare as you enter the shed.

Some of the paintings have been turned to the wall. Others lie buried under twenty or more small sketches that litter the worktable or spill over, from time to time, onto the waterlogged planks at the center of the sloping floor.

> *The subject is riderless. A black coat without markings of any kind, save for the gray streak that runs from the nostrils to the space between the eyes. The forelegs are crossed rather casually on a boulder or on the remains of a ruined wall. The*

> *subject appears lost in some vague media-*
> *tion as he leans up against the rubble (a*
> *pose not characteristic of the quadruped).*
> *The work is at least a hundred years old;*
> *the setting, a desert landscape within sight*
> *of an oasis. The clouds have gone from*
> *white to ocher. The earth is of an unnatural*
> *flatness. No sign of a dune, nor even the*
> *slightest undulation on the horizon. The*
> *sand—it seems to be sand—appears in a*
> *crystalline state, riddled with the same*
> *network of cracks that mars the surface*
> *whenever the portrait is turned to catch*
> *the light. A thick coating of varnish has, by*
> *now, given the scene an antique finish and*
> *sapped most of the natural color it might*
> *at one time have possessed.*

I said grapeshot. That, too, was a mistake. Yet another meta-
phor, and since there's no getting rid of them ... what I meant to say
was that it *felt* like grapeshot or, more precisely, the idea—I'd kept
it hidden even from myself until that very moment—of how
grapeshot has to sound when it strikes the helmet that happens to be
resting upon one's head. It's just something that occurred to me at
the time, of no real importance. But I won't take it back. I thought
it had to be grapeshot (after all, I was slipping off the ledge) until I
realized that the geologist must have somehow closed the distance
between us and had stopped to ... I was under the impression, once
I had regained my equilibrium, that he was doing it deliberately—
the geologist, I mean—that he was gathering samples, pulling
berries off the frozen umbels that grow out of the crags, and tossing
the inferior specimens away. Two or three of these pellets stung me
as I continued my descent. I reached the next ledge and was able to
swing myself down out of the way through a narrow opening in the
ice. I barely managed to squeeze through. The opposing walls had
almost come together. I thought I must be near the bottom, and as
I kicked my crampons more deliberately into the crust —I went
slowly now—I gradually became aware that the ice wall was sloping

at an angle of about sixty degrees from the horizontal. Once again it became impossible to say how close I had come to the bottom of the ravine. The wall was smoother there. There were no more crags. No signs of frozen vegetation. It was impossible now to drive any more pitons into the ice. I could no longer see the basalt pillars; their green traces had disappeared beneath an impenetrable white mass. I could no longer afford to tilt my head in any way that threw the lamp's reflection back full on my eyes; its contrast to the darkness was so great that a sudden flash in the sheen of the ice would burn blue suns into my retina. I'd have to wait for the suns to purple before I made my next move. It was so cold. I thought my breath was going to freeze in the air and leave me with a clot of ice stuffed in my nose and mouth, reaching into my lungs. The angle of the wall became even more acute. Soon I was at forty-five degrees, hanging on as best I could. Five or six steps down. Thirty degrees. It was too much. I had to let go.

REEL #1   ○ ❑ ❑ ❑ ❑ ○   PHILOSOPHER

: : : : yes all right I'll try to keep my voice down this time : : : : : hello : : : is it on? : : : : : they want me to say something about him : : : : : : : he was usually very quiet : : : kept to his room for hours at a time what? : : : : : : yes I'm coming to it let me tell it in my own way : : : : : it was in his room : : that study of his : : : one night he locked himself in I could hear the clap of his hooves on the floorboards back and forth back and forth all night long : : : he didn't like to have a rug in there : : he said it made him feel somehow off kilter : : but anyway when he finally came out he looked tired : : his eyes drooped and he was in such a sweat that I went to get the saddlecloth and threw it over him before he had time to open his mouth oh I can tell you he was excited : : he wanted to say something but I still don't understand what he was talking about : : : : : he was getting old I can't say how long we'd been married he was in the study most of the time he spent with me : : locked up in there alone I'm not complaining but it's just that he came home so seldom and to go and lock himself in like that I practically had to push his food in under the door : : : : : : don't believe what the others tell you I was his wife all right all

*right I was just getting to it : : : : : : he looked at me as if he'd
never seen me before and he said : : let me try to get it right : : :
: : The sun : : The sun is a second moon : : The sun is merely
a second moon empty of shadows : : yes that's it those are his exact
words I'm sure of it : : : : : anyway what*

Of the ground, what came into the pool of light was mostly the
color ocher, a patch of crag-ridden waste foxed with brown speckles
and gray villous weeds; weeds matted under a thick, transparent
sheet of ice. I had fallen maybe two or three feet. As I lay there
gasping for breath a freezing pain bit into my lungs. For a time I
couldn't move at all. The mist rose off the ravine floor, it enveloped
everything; the bottom of the icewall lay somewhere behind it. I had
resigned myself to a quick death. Impact with the ground had come
almost immediately. It was enough of a fall to knock the wind out
of me, nothing more. My helmet must have spun around on the ice
for half a minute —I remember the intermittent flash of a beacon
cutting through the fog out of the corner of my eye, at first the only
thing of which I was conscious. When I could breathe again, I began
to crawl toward the beacon. My icehammers were stuck in the
ravine wall; it was useless to go back after them, I had already lost
all sense of direction. I still had the ax. When I got to my helmet—
I would seem to have been crawling in that general direction,
heading toward the beam of slivered light a few feet away, for an
excessively long interval of time —I put it on and immediately
began to chip away at the icecrust in order to take a small sample of
what lay beneath. The dull metallic echo, caroming off the mist and
the hidden icewalls, became almost hypnotic as I raised and lowered
my ax in a uniform tempo, curbing the force of each drive into the
icefloor just to prolong my task, to give myself some time to let my
mind wander, time not to have to think at all. I should have noticed
the sound of approaching footsteps. In any case, whoever it was
could have fallen in step with the constant ring of my ax—it seemed
to obliterate all other noises. I bent forward, trying to dislodge a clod
of freckled earth with the ax handle when, from nowhere, the blunt
toes of a pair of calfskin boots appeared beneath the hem of a black
woolen cloak.

From the upper lefthand corner, the halo of a new moon lights up the peaks of what few clouds remain above the sycamores. The subject's head appears lower down, a little to the right of center in the labyrinth, peeping out from between two perfectly straight tree trunks; it gives off a light all its own, a milky ethereal candescence. The eyes are white, devoid of iris and pupil. Though completely hidden in underbrush, the length of the body is nonetheless evidenced by highlights cast on clusters of leaves, bushes, tree trunks; the blades of grass are lit as though from a string of white crêpe Chinese lanterns hung out of vision to replace the formless or nonexistent body. The bit has fallen from between the subject's teeth. A saddle horn is visible just above where his back would be if you could make it out behind the bushes and leaves that hide the lower branches. Aside from that there is nothing to disprove the theory that one sees, in this work, a disembodied head stuffed with excelsior by some enterprising taxidermist and fixed at the neck to the hidden side of one of the sycamore trunks. If we follow the above premise to its logical conclusion, the "smile" becomes all the more disconcerting in that it seems to contradict the general appearance of the head as something altogether artificial – indeed, it has the consistency of a wad of cotton candy. Or maybe it's a joke, two men in a horse suit, as the engineer has suggested.

When the face comes down it comes all too slowly, incomplete, the tip of a nose and two glints where the eyes are set deep in the cowl's shadow, as though the cowl detaches head from body. Mist lingers between the hidden face and the hem of the cloak.

The figure makes a sign for me to rise. I don't move.

A withered hand grasps my pick by the adz and drags me several hundred feet across the icefloor to a place where the fog has lifted.

My headlamp (whether I am still wearing the lamp, or whether the light comes from another source, I can't say now) brings two more figures out of the darkness. Their cowls uncover brittle shags of hair made white in contrast to the cloaks that wrap their bodies from chin to foot.

The figure with me also lowers her cowl. It's getting warmer. She has a sad old face.

REEL #2 ○ ❑ ❑ ❑ ❑ ○ NATURE ARCHITECT

/nsatiable : : especially when it came to th/ /_____ /
/ver letting himself go that far : : : : : no : : once he'd drawn
up the final plans there was no living with him : : : you'd think that
with a wine-trough he wouldn't have to be so sloppy : : : com/
_____ /o there instead just to see how work was pro-
gressing on the generator : : : : : : he must have realized from
the very beginning that something was needed : : call it a
mechanical assurance if you like : : so he had this special place
built just to house the generator : : : : from the outside it looked
like a scaled-down version of the Bourse whatever that is he was
always saying The Bourse the Bourse what inspiration to make it
resemble the Bourse : : : Even if they get this far they'll never
suspect : : I can always open one or two of the pipes before they
reach the bottom : : : : but of course it never worked : : after
all here we are : : I don't think he ever finished it at any rate I never
saw it : : : I got to look at the drawings though : : : a little square
at the bottom with spidery tentacles running up through a cross-
section of the lithosphere that's what they all looked like : : each
drawing a numbered variation on the ones that had come before :
: : : for long periods of time I never knew where he was : : :
he'd leave his sketches lying about all over the place and tell me not
to touch anything : : : six months : : once he stayed away for
nearly a year I don't know : : I never questioned him : : : I was
afraid he might have trampled me to death no it wasn't right
between us for a long time : : : I'd go out alone you know it's

warmer there : : not like it is up here : : : not nearly as bright
either how do you stand it? : : : : : : : : : what? : : : : c'mon
speak up : : : : : you don't want the machine to hear you is that
it? : : : : : oh the mist : : no there isn't any mist just an even
deep blue light : : : he claimed to have built the machine that makes
the light : : who kn/ /_____/ /f you really want to know :
: : why all this fuss about the light? : : : : : well all right he calls
it the Grand Refulgent Dome : : :/ /_____/
/getation : : nothing like you've got here everything is dead where
are the colors that give life to nature? : : no we've got it much better
: : : the organisms never fade : : they're in abundance : : pink
and yellow pods streaked with blue veins like miniature umbrellas
stuck close to the ground : : : you can sit on them : : they yield
quite easily to the contours of any posterior : : : the trunks of the
trees are smooth and porous like human skin : : they secrete a mild
perfume that makes the air breathable : : : when the trees die the
dream is over : : we'll have to live here above ground like the
ancestors : : : he made every one of those trees : : : even if the
generator didn't work according to plan the trees at least will never
die : : : : : the flowers open to expel their bubbles : : they take
in air as we do and then exhale their weightless pearls : : : : the
bubbles have a milky skin : : a membrane thin as a hair : : : the
sheen moves like rainbow-smoke beneath the surface : : you turn
them over gently in your hand and the smoke forms little pictures
like the one I have here : : : see? : : : : : : : : : :/

Her zigzag scar reminds me of a streak of pink lightning.

She took her place with the other two beside the mouth of the crater. Outside the circle—an invisible barrier delimited by jagged earth-pillars the color of sifted ash—the mist billowed into the ground.

I stood on dry land. The ice was gone.

What had been beneath the ice remained: sand, hairlike weeds sprouting around my ankles. A dim light, filtered from behind the crater ridge, made blue outlines of the three old heads. The rim of silt was blue where the light spilled over.

It was only then, after I had taken in the careworn features of each woman's face, that I began to feel a slight vibration under my feet, a faint rumbling in the crater depths.

The technique, however contrived, lends a nonethe-less forbidding intimacy to the otherwise banal set-ting, putting it, at first glance, almost beyond the pale of recognition. There is only a mere suggestion of form, a gradual yet precise range of monotones—the magnetic pull of a light toward which all imaginary lines converge. The sitter, dressed in the uniform of a Prussian student, reclines at ease upon a chaise longue. He is depicted in the act of lighting a fine meerschaum pipe, the glow of whose rekindled ash shows up, somewhat artificially, in the monocle screwed to his left eye. This detail, and perhaps the idea of the pipe itself, might rest with the sitter rather than with the artist, since one of the stretchers in back of the canvas bears the inscription, in German: Commissioned of the painter H. Franz von Schliebentaup, Naumberg 1849. *The sitter reclines, in the ill-lit corner of a sumptuous study, before a wall of bookshelves all but obliterated by the screen of ballooning pipe smoke. Above the smoke, in a shadow that deepens toward the borders of the picture, a portrait-bust of Schopenhauer reposes on one of the uppermost shelves, discernible only because the attention that the artist has given to its every detail clearly exceeds that given to anything else in the work. The sitter, if we exclude his rather absurd monocle (which may have, in any case, been an afterthought) and his beautiful pipe, is, by contrast with the bust, merely sketched in among the other highlights. His head and body take up a surprisingly small portion of the overall composition. An ebony forelock peeps out from beneath the vizorless kepi. The face is raw umber. Sienna-red markings continue down from around the eyes in tiny flecks the shape of crescents along the whole length of the muzzle.*

A perceptible resonance . . .

As I reached the edge of the crater, I felt the soles of my boots give way to a sudden pull of centrifugal wind. I got down on my knees and peered over the rim into a tunnel that looked as though it ran straight through the center of the earth. The warm wind came to me in steady, circular gusts. Modulations far beyond the farthest point my eyes could read held me in thrall. I let myself be drawn into the whirlpool.

It was impossible to say precisely when the blue light began to recede into the depths. Little by little the outer confines of the tunnel were going black—a blackness pitched downward into the absence of all trace of blue, toward the matrix of a deep, vertiginous spiral. In less than a minute, what had all too quickly become a remote star vanished.

REEL #3   ◯ ❑ ❑ ❑ ❑ ◯   **LOVER**

/cking as much by then if you really must know I' m not ashamed to say it : : not any more at least : : : I may have a foot in the grave but I can still recall the early days : : : : : oh yes : : since you asked about the Bourse I' ve been thinking : : I used to pass it often enough on my daily walks it' s a wonder I didn' t remember it sooner : : the inscription on the pediment it reads CABALLVS EST SOL INFERVS : : : : : ah you don' t understand isn' t there anyone around here who speaks Latin? : : : : : : all right it means THE HORSE IS THE LOWER SUN that' s close enough and it' s all I can tell you I don' t know why he had it put up there I never went in myself : : guess I was never that curious about it it wasn' t really that interesting and I already had plenty to do wh/ /_____ /

/mpossible to get to the tunnel without first having reached the crater : : : if we had wanted to kill your friend we' d have done it then : : after all we did give ourselves up we led you to where he had fallen : : it was his own fault we could have left him there to die you know we didn' t have to tell you anything : : : he must have been a bit delirius : : he was leaning over the edge and he fell no one pushed him : : do you think we' d have given ourselves up so easily if we thought you' d susp

/

/

/*to ask him what he wanted oh at first there wasn't much ceremony
about it he'd just coax me gently onto the bed with his hooves : :
: I used to brace my feet in his stirrups : : : : : he never got
rough or anything like that unless I was in the mood for it but as time
wore on : : as time wore on it became more and more : : difficult
: : : he'd want me to dress up in boots and : : and a black lace
corset and I had to strut about the room slapping a riding crop
against my thigh and shouting commands in German : : : on those
occasions he would turn out in full military regalia harness and all
and trot about the room in time with the beating of my crop : : :
: : time passed : : : my costumes became more and more
extravagant : : : I wound up dressed as the Queen of Sheba : :
I had to get him to clear the bed three times in a row without grazing
the sheets with his hooves before he was worked-up enough to do
anything : : : : you look a little disappointed : : well I'll tell
you it doesn't get any better : : : the next step of course was : :
: : : : : well what could I do I was his wife after all : : and
I thought maybe it would : : it might uh : : you know maybe it would
bring him around : : restore his : : : : : : : yes : : well
I suppose it always ends with perversion when you get like that : :
: : : gradually we both came to realize it was no use going on : : :
he resigned himself : : : : : : : we've grown old together he
and I : : : but we were young once : : : : : he was a good mount
then : : : : : : : his eyes : : : already the night : : : : no
: : I won't say any more I don't want to turn it off : : turn it off
! : : : you're all fools if you think my husband will ever let you take
him alive no you'll never take him never do you und/*

Behind me the tunnel was pitched in darkness. I must have been
walking for a long time.

The entrance had dwindled to a flickering saffron dot.

1975

Cellophane Sky

Judy Katz-Levine

I was riding the bus. One of those ice days when the ground is hard cellophane. I always choose the single blue seats. I look out the window, watching jeeps and Volvos buck, pass the health food store. Two men got onto the bus, went for the seat in front of mine, but on the other side of the aisle. Both wearing dirty brown coats, both kind of rocking and falling into the seats. The one by the aisle was grinning all the time. I looked away so they wouldn't notice me. The one by the window started talking and as he spoke his friend would smile, smile wider.

"My blood is made of formaldehyde, half formaldehyde half blood. They got me from the morgue. They revived me. I don't know my name. Maybe I'm John Devirges. Maybe I'm not. Maybe I'm Albert Shapiro. Maybe I'm not. I live in Roslindale, I live in Hyde Park. I live in Ohio. My blood is half formaldehyde. They had to revive me."

There were seven of us on the bus. We all pretended we didn't hear him. He was shouting. His face was red, there was a rash on his neck, and he was fat, not too fat, but not thin.
"Maybe I'm a thousand names. I can't remember my name. I can't remember. Maybe I'm Wally. Maybe I'm not."

He was rocking back and forth. "I'm an outpatient. The doctor says 'How goes it?' I'm going to the V.A. hospital. I graduated. I'm an outpatient, now. I go to get my pills."
His partner was smiling. The bus stopped. The nameless man stood up with his friend, who held his elbow, and escorted him to the door, still smiling.

Then it seemed too quiet as the bus oozed to the corner of South Huntington. I got off there. I went into a Spanish sub shop and ordered some kind of meat pie and two chocolate chip cookies. The sky was like cellophane, now. I had a long walk ahead of me.

Bo

Stephen Dixon

One day I'm just not in my right mind. That's about the best way
I can put it. I might have felt pretty bad other days but this day on
the subway I'm really feeling things aren't right in my head and I'm
definitely not in my right mind. That's closer. I'll begin when and
where. I'm heading uptown. The express. IND. Months ago. Heading to my girlfriend's house. Not a girl, a woman. Her daughter's the
girl. I got my valise for the weekend. My rough work clothes, my
good clothes and the clothes I got on. Also some shorts and sneakers
in the valise so I can run once a day the two days I'll be there. I'm
going to help on her house. Fix up the basement with her. Plaster the
floor, point up the brick walls as she says. What do I know from
pointing? On the phone the night before she told me. Got a call from
her. Big surprise: "Come up, all is forgiven, I love you very much.
You must hate me by now the way I go back and forth in my
emotions with you, but now I know how wrong I was and that you're
the man for me. Leonore misses you too." Leonore's her daughter.
I call her Lee. So does her dad. "All right," I said, "all is forgiven,
and probably forgotten. I love you very much too, so when should
I come up?"

"Right now if it was possible.   But you won't take off unless
you're really sick, so come up tomorrow after work."

"All right. I'll catch the 6:10 bus."

"Just take the subway to the bus station and I'll drive down and
pick you up there."

"Why bother? I'll take the bus from the bus station and be in
your cute little town by seven."

That's what it is. Cute. She too. Her daughter also. Their house,
the town, the main street and surrounding countryside, all cute.
"Till then, sweetheart," and I said "Same here," but felt a little as if
I didn't know if I was doing the right thing going up there. I'd
thought it was over between us. Glad it's not. All right, I'll go. I
want to be with her. I love them both. So I go to sleep, to work the
next day and half past five I'm on the A train that's to take me to the
bus station at George Washington Bridge.   But on the subway I

suddenly feel peculiar. I don't know what it is or where from. People looking at me strangely, maybe me at them too. The newspapers. Talk of war, other countries' wars, sex, murder, scandals, gossip, all kinds of statistics and reports. People reading. Magazines too. The subway ads seem strange and horrible to me too. Everyone seems exhausted. Everything seems stupid and inhuman, like none of us should or don't belong. Like I especially don't belong. Subway rocking side to side. Screeching noises of passing trains and our train and whistles too. People pushing, some don't. Getting off, on. I'm standing. Need a seat. None. Crowded. I'm feeling crowded in by everyone and it seems everything and almost want to scream. I hold one back. I'm feeling scared. The subway. Where's it going? Uptown the passing local stations say. Where am I going? Rochelle's, or I'm not so sure. I'm sweating. Back, neck and face. I wish I was there already where I'm going. Rochelle's, but I don't know if I belong there now. With her. Here. Anywhere in the world in fact. I have to get off. Maybe it's some different kind of flu. I better wait till the train stops. It stops. I run upstairs. It's not the bus station stop. That one I know where everyone from the front cars jam themselves in to get on the bus-station stairs. I have to call someone. I get the wrong number.

"No Rochelle here. What number you want?"

"I forget."

"Did you know what number when you dialed?"

"I'm not too sure."

"No wonder you got the wrong number. Please don't call again?"

"How can I if I don't know your number?"

"Right."

"I'm sorry. I'm not feeling too good right now, honestly. I was calling a friend for help." But he's hung up. I go through my wallet. I can't find her number. I always had it memorized. I know the area code is 914. Once I wrote her number down. When I first met her. On a library card. Now I remember. That I wrote it down. But that library card expired. I got a new one last year. Didn't put her number on the new one because I remembered it by then. Whose? Rochelle's. Rochelle Parker. 122 West Milner St., Piermont, New York. I dial information. I give information Rochelle's name, address and town. She tells me to dial out-of-town information and gives me the number. I do. I get her number. I get Rochelle. "Rochelle, something crazy has happened. I suddenly feel all mixed up and so out of it you wouldn't believe it and I don't know why. Please come and get me."

"What's wrong?"

"I just told you. My head. I feel crazy."

"You do sound a little crazy. You aren't just joking? You're not calling from town?"

"I'm on 168th Street. Please come. I'm not kidding."

"I will."

I give her the address. I'm sitting on the cover of a garbage can when she comes. My valise I must have left in the train. I don't care. Work clothes, good clothes, as long as I got some clothes on. I get in the car and she drives. She says "What's wrong?" "Rochelle," I say, hugging her at a stoplight, wanting to be held. She takes me to her home, puts me to bed. I stay there for two days. Lee's away with her dad and his new wife. Rochelle feeds me broth, tea and toast, saying it's probably only a very bad Asian type flu I have which sometimes does weird things to the mind. "That's what I think too," but by Sunday she says "Maybe we're both wrong." She takes me to her G. P. He examines and talks to me and recommends a special public hospital in the county. He calls and they say for me to come by later that afternoon. Just before we leave for the hospital, Lee and her dad drive up to the house.

"You going so soon?"

"Afraid I have to."

"But you never go till Monday morning. And Dad got me two new card decks just so you and I can play Spit."

"I'll explain later," Rochelle says to them both.

The two admitting doctors ask me what I think is wrong. I tell them I don't know, it's tough to explain, I'm sure it started on the subway, but I don't feel as if I can go on with my life the way it is, at one point I thought it was just the world in general, the whole world, I don't know how other people are able to face it, but right now I can't. I feel terrible, not suicidal, just scared, confused, closed in, claustrophobic, strange feelings about everything in my head that make me sweat something awful and my body shake right down to my legs which I've never had anything quite like before. They say they understand. I say "You do?" Would I put myself in here for two to four weeks, maybe more, but a minimum of ten days? I look at Rochelle. She says "I think it's the best thing you can do." We kiss and she leaves. They give me drugs, a complete physical exam, a room to share with a very quiet man, want me to see a therapist twice a day just to speak. I tell her it suddenly came on me on the subway. She says it suddenly didn't and has probably been coming on for years, maybe since early childhood. "My childhood was great, so don't give me that."

"You might have thought and still think your childhood was great and no doubt many parts of it were, but let's talk about it some more tomorrow, okay?"

We talk about my dead parents and older brother who died in a bathtub. I say I loved all three very much. She says I may have loved them and very much but also could have feared them very much too. Not true, I say, as they never did anything like even lift a pinky finger to me to make me feel afraid. Maybe you're right, she says, or maybe you've forgotten or don't want to think about it and haven't wanted to for twenty or so years, but let's talk about it some more this evening, okay?

About my ex-wife, child in Georgia, Rochelle, Lee, friends, schools, religion, work and sex habits. Past compulsions to get lots of attention, later desires for almost complete goody-goodiness and anonymity. "When did you change?" "When my brother passed out and drowned?" "That doesn't jell with what I've got down you already said, and the chronology." "Then I don't know. Or I'm still not sure. But I don't care how much I'm not sweating anymore, I'm even more confused now than when I first came in here and don't see how all this talk's going to make me improve."

They put me on a special diet. Try another drug as the one I've been taking turns out to be bad for my kidneys. Ask if I'll consent to staying a minimum of ten more days. I have to phone my boss and tell him I won't be coming in for two more weeks and he says then in that case he's going to have to let me go.

"All right then, you want to be unfair, be unfair. I'll be in this Monday nine on the nose."

"Tell you the truth, I got a new guy who does twice the job as you for a lot less starting money. And you took off too many sick days when I knew you didn't have to and weren't such a hot worker, so maybe you better not come back at all."

"Now you're making me mad. Everybody there knows I never took off when I wasn't absolutely dying, and for my extra overtime for the company I never once thought to be paid. Look, I've been told to express my feelings more so I'm expressing them, for you know yourself you always said I was a hundred percent straight and honest and one of your hardest workers and for that praise I never had to ask. 'Damn good worker' were your damn words."

"You must've been hearing things then too. By the way, what's your room number so some of your former fellow employees can send you a bouquet."

"What's that crack supposed to mean?"

"You don't like flowers? Then a joint card with all their signatures or maybe a basket of fruit. They told me to ask in case you had to stay."

"Nobody there wants to send me any card or fruit and you know it."

"They don't? I'll tell them that and you can be certain they won't. Take care of yourself, Bo."

"Sure, you give a damn. Just don't forget to put down that you fired me, you cheap bastard, for when I get out of here I want to walk into some unemployment checks."

"No skin off my pecker, tough guy, but for reasons of your kind of sickness or just any, I don't know if they give," and he hangs up.

Rochelle comes every other day around six. Sits with me. Says "You look better and seem to act better, you feel better too?" No. "Then you don't want to stay here longer?" Yes. I stay three more months. They give me plenty of pills, see that I swallow them and hope I'll continue to take my prescribed medicine once I leave here, "though remember, don't mix them with alcohol or you can die." After the three months I don't feel that much better but think it's time to go. My hospital coverage is up. My ex-wife writes she's ready to get the court to take away all fatherly rights from me for either unsoundness of mind or non-child support. Rochelle has already told me she met another man and I shouldn't try and contact her anymore, and nobody I know takes her visitor place. Lee sends me a handmade get-well card once a week right up until the time I leave.

"You know, you really aren't sufficiently cured yet," the therapist says and I say "What can I tell you—I haven't the money to stay."

"You can readmit yourself involuntarily and become a ward of the state, which in residency terms means you'd have to stay here till we say you can go."

"No, I think from now on, with a more responsible and positive attitude and meaningful job and more openness to people and no expectations about what I deserve out of life or preconceptions of what normalcy is . . ."

I'm given a month's supply of medicine and names of a few free group sessions in the city and return to my old neighborhood. My furnished room's been rented and what belongings I have are with the super downstairs. "Keep them," I say. "For I think if I'm really going to change my way of living and looking at things, I'm going to need a new apartment in another setting with better furnishings and wardrobe."

"If you change your mind by tomorrow morning, they'll be out front on the street."

I call up a friend. "Bobo, how are you, I heard what happened, tough luck, pal, as we always thought you were sitting on top of the world and had it made."

"Truth is, I'm still not that sure how it happened, but I think I know how it won't again. I'm looking for a place to stay for a short while till I get back on my feet."

"You want me to put you up here?"

"I'll be direct; that's what I had in mind."

"Can't do. Booked solid with sweethearts all this week. Why don't you try Ken?"

Ken and Mary. Of course. Nice couple. Old friends. Ken says "Fine with me, let me speak to Mary." Comes back on the phone: "She says no deal."

"Okay. No problem."

"It's nothing to do with where you been. Just she's still got this gripe against you for the way you treated Claire."

"What do you mean? Claire slept around and kicked me out of the house and wanted the divorce, not me."

"Listen, they speak on the phone. It's not only your missing kid payments for most of the year, but also the slow, subtle and maybe unintentional way Claire says you nearly drove her mad. She's got the shrink bills and mental bruises to prove it. Even your little girl had to go to one for a child."

"Could be true. Maybe I forgot how bad I was or like they say, repressed it so I'd forget. But I've already sent them most of my cash, just as I'm going to make good on all my old debts and not return to my mistakes and alibis of the past, so believe me everything's going to work out great for me and tell Mary I can understand how she feels."

"That's the spirit. Look, try Burleigh. His lodger left last week."

I phone Burleigh. Says "Sure, for one-fifty a month."

"I'm broke. Give me time to get a job and pay."

"Money on the line, Bo—I've got to live off what I get for rent. If it's not you then from a singles renting agency I can get a guy or girl for two and a half bills a month."

Several other people. Finally a friend of a friend who I heard might be renting says I can sleep on the floor for the night, but that's the best she can do.

Following day I'm out early looking for work. "In these times? Where you been? Factories are folding left and right or moving out of here, city's in hock up to its ears. Take a dishwasher job if you can find one, because with your skills, experience and education, that's about the best you'll get for the next two years." Unemployment says "If you are eligible for insurance, not for another three weeks." She wants me to fill out more forms. I say "Just a second, got to go to the mensroom," stomachful of nerves from the lines and ugly walls and all her questions and suspicions and I leave the building through the rear. I'm in a spot. Few dollars in my wallet. No likeable relatives with spare beds or money, friends with anything to lend. I get on the subway to try and convince that woman to let me stay two more nights on her floor. Suddenly I'm confused. Difficult to explain. Short of breath, face popping out sweat, agitated, woozy, symptoms, a little depressed. I take two of my pills dry just as I was told to do with outside emergencies when I'm feeling this distressed. For a few seconds I think they're stuck in my windpipe and try coughing them up. "Ach! Ach!" People looking at me with that look what's with him? Newspapers, magazines. Not so sure where I'm heading or presently am. Rush hour and with each door closing we're more crammed in. Horrible photos of victims, survivors, oppressors, refugees. Local passing stations going the opposite way I want telling me I'm traveling uptown. Next ride's a long one and when we stop I shove my way out to slap my face and blow my nose and breathe. Bags? Have any? On the platform I say "Say, buddy, not so fast, will you, for can you tell me—" but he runs upstairs. "Miss?" She too. Now nobody. I sit on a bench. Station attendant approaches same time as the next express. He says something but I don't hear him past the train's screeching wheels. Broom and dustpan with a long stick at the end of it, sweeping up wrappers and papers, dumping everything into the trashcan by my bench. Doors open, close, people breeze by, platform empty again.

"Anything the matter?" he says.

"Ah, so you noticed."

"Too much to drink?"

"Too much of everything, but not drink. I can't."

"Bad news if that was to me happening," and he laughs and sweeps.

"I'm actually saying," but I'll be brief. He: "What's it then, drugs?" Me: "Drugs, yes, but hospital drugs for a manic depressed." Talk of drugs leads to thoughts of where I got them. After a long discussion about our mutual social and psychological problems and many of them similar, I ask him to call the hospital, give him the number from my head and change. He says on the phone "This the hospital. Not a hospital," to me.

"Whose number I give?"

"What number is this? The man who told me to call wants to know. Who's the man? Person wants to know who you are." I give my name. He give it and says to me "Says to put you on."

"Bo, this is Rochelle. What are you up to now?"

But I said I'd be brief. She eventually comes to get me. First she says "Why'd you call?" I say "I was calling the hospital to go back." Operator wants more change. Neither the attendant or I have it so Rochelle takes the number and calls back. For a while we can't speak because of the train noise. "I said would you please come here to drive me to the hospital?" The attendant tells her how to get to the station once she's on either deck of the George Washington Bridge. In an hour she's come. Hugs me, won't let me kiss her, says "car's doubleparked so let's make it quick."

Takes my arm and we go. Her boyfriend's behind the wheel. Once across the bridge and on the parkway I say, "I'm really feeling much better now and don't want to be anymore of an inconvenience, so why don't you let me off right here." He says "We phoned the hospital after Rochelle spoke to you before and they said to bring you up there soon as we can."

"Well that's what you're doing then."

"You don't think it's for the best?" she says.

"I'm sleepy, Rochelle."

Next thing I know she's tapping me on the shoulder as we arrive.

I Always Carry A Gun

Danny Antonelli

I always carry a gun.

I haven't used it on anybody yet. But I always got it with me because this is a bad city and a bad world in general and anyway it's the people that make it bad because they don't want to put up with all the bullshit attached to getting things. And I can't blame those guys who are starving and need to feed because I know it's hard times. But it's hard times for all of us together and anyway it's never the guy in the limousine who gets knocked over his head or raped or what-have-you. It's me. Guys like me. I gotta walk to work mornings because the goddamn busses are always full and anyway the traffic's so congealed you'd get there later. And I wouldn't own a car because it gets stolen and the cops don't give a damn even if they get lucky and find it before it gets painted and sold again. And anyway the cops are all rotten and after all they don't want to get shot or starve either and the way things go you know they must worry about it. Especially if I only carry my gun to protect me from those creeps along the street because all they want is a couple of bucks for their next fix you can image how a cop worries. I don't blame them for shooting before they ask questions. But they don´t really care because there's nothing they can do about solving all the criminals who walk around free and even in jail they live like kings, TV and movies and food and even all the drugs they need because everyone's corrupt. Me, I'm not corrupt but I get what I can when it falls my way. It's normal. Because I work at selling clothes, suits mainly but we got shirts and there's even a shoe department but I never go near there because if you ever wanted to meet a disgusting bunch of crooks you should meet a shoe salesman. Me, I try to do my customers right and get them into suits that look good and fit right, even the portly guy, because then the place gets a name and they come back to me and it's a way to make friends and stay in good with the management. I've had the same guys some of them come back for years. But when they buy a whole outfit, shirt, tie, three-piece suit, socks, they drop a hint about shoes and if I know them some time I tell them to go to a good shoe store because then the suit will look even better. But if I don't know them much or the floor manager's around then I point them in the direction and say We have a fine shoe department just over there behind those pillars. Of course it's a lie because the shoes are bad and the salesmen are worse but it's part of my job and anyway the customer's gotta beware. Isn't that it? So I guess that in that way I'm sometimes corrupt but I never steal. There's been a few salesmen have passed through here who thought they could get away with some sharp deals like selling clothes to a buddy who doesn't really pay and then walks out with all the stuff and later sells it uptown somewhere and they split the take. But they always get caught. If not their very first time then eventually because they're greedy and we have lots of store detectives who look like customers and come in and watch how things work and eventually everybody gets caught. Of course sometimes there's Sales and I put some nice things aside for myself and when the Sale's over and the unsold stuff's gonna be shipped out the floor manager always knocks off an extra 20% and I take the stuff. I like to dress good but it's not safe to walk around looking too nice so I usually wear my regular grey suit on the street and change into one of the latest style coats we got once I get to work. My closet at home is full of real nice things and sometimes I wear them around the house. I don't go out much weekends or nights, sometimes to to a movie, but I watch TV and read The News. Only all I read is the crime section because I want to be ready to do what I have to do when the time comes. On TV they show dead guys sometimes, or bloodstains on the sidewalk and they're never red even though my TV's got good color. The stains are always kind of black. I saw a dog dead once on the street and it was a sunny day and the blood had come out of his mouth and was all out in front of him in a big splash and was orange. Bright orange like dayglo paints. And I remember thinking that he must have died slowly because there was so much blood because once I read somewhere, or somebody told me, how when you die everything inside you stops including the blood. But I guess human blood is black. Or so dark red it looks black on TV. And I wonder if when I shoot mine it'll get on TV and I'll be interviewed by that blond girl who always seems to be on the spot when really awful things happen. Sandy something is her name. Or will I have to go downtown for questioning. I want to make sure I

know what to do when it happens because I wouldn´t want anyone
to think it was anything like murder or something because basically
I'm a nice guy and don't hate anybody, not even Rube Styles who
is the guy who married Jenny. I should hate him because I think I
was in love with her but I don't. He was always better at sports than
me in high school and she was a cheerleader and I guess that I didn't
have a chance anyway. They moved out to Wisconsin or something
and he wouldn't be on the street trying to rob me anyway, and I
would recognize him I think even if he was. He might not remember
me too well because he was always on teams and in clubs and I just
stayed in the background though I came in second in a chess
tournament once. But he never played chess. And I don't play
anymore either. And I've lost a little weight and a lot of hair up front.
But it makes me look smarter, more intellectual, or that's what one
of my customers said once. But maybe he didn't mean it. Anyway
I'm not a bad guy and I wouldn't go shooting anybody just for fun.
Only when they threaten me. You know it's gonna happen. I mean
it's happening all the time and it's gonna be my turn one day but I
won't put up with it. If he has a gun or something then I'll just wait
until he turns around. I don't necessarily want to kill him but it's
probably better that way because otherwise they get out of hospital
and out of jail and they've got memories and even if you move or
change jobs they have those friends and can find out all sorts of
things. And I don't want to change jobs because I'm happy where
I am, with seniority and all, and in 10 or 15 years–my choice–I can
retire and maybe I'll move out to some small place in the country
and be happy like those people are supposed to be. Though it would
be kind of late for me to go hunting for a wife. All these young girls
want is to go out dancing all the time and to take their drugs and
spend my money. And anyway where I work all I meet is men. But
I never felt queer so that doesn't help. Even though at school once
some of the tough sports guys tried to start a rumor about me because
I didn't get any girlfriends. But Jenny liked me. And we used to take
the bus home together sometimes and sit together if there was room.
She always talked a lot about places she was gonna go when she left
school and I thought about how nice it would be to be with her. And
she told me how she was impressed because I was so good at math
and she was sure I'd grow up to be a scientist sending men to the
moon and things. But in our senior year her folks moved to a new

apartment on the West Side and she took a different bus home and I didn't get great grades on my college boards and after Dad got laid off I decided it would be better for us if I got a job. And the managers are real impressed because I've been able to stick it out there through thick and thin and it's paying off I guess because I live OK and I've got plenty of people to talk to at work and even though my apartment's small, it's cheap, and since Mom died it's been a lot less trouble because even if I miss my parents sometimes in a strange way I'm glad they're not around to see me because I think they always secretly expected me to be a doctor or a lawyer or something and when they realized I wasn't they got kind of deflated and that's the way they'd always look at me, deflated, and though they never said anything I think they would have enjoyed a grandson or something. At least Dad would've before his stroke because he always used to take me out for walks in the park on Sunday afternoons, winter, summer, didn't matter how hot or how cold and he missed doing that I think because those last few years before his final stroke he'd always bring back memories about the days when I was a kid. And Mom would get all nervous and try and distract him because she knew he would get upset when he remembered he couldn't walk any more and he could barely talk. But it's not really my fault for not trying because after Jenny there was one of the girls in the stock room who I went to movies with a few times and to dinner once in a nice restaurant but she didn't know which fork to use for the fish and she wanted coke with her meal and even though I'm not a gourmet I know as much as you don't eat fish with coke and even that part with the fork would have been OK otherwise because even I had to learn that. And maybe I could have taught her to drink white wine or beer with it but she got fired for smoking among the cardboard boxes which is strictly forbidden because of the hazard and I don't know if I would have liked to live with somebody who smoked all the time like she did. Linda. My mother would have disapproved because she was only a stock girl but when we had a kid she would have been won over like all of them are. I guess I'd make a poor father since I'm not too good at sports but I'd take him out walking all the time. Though I don't go to the park anymore myself. It's too dangerous in the evenings and on the weekends it's so crowded with kids that you always have to be on your toes that you don't get beaned by a ball or one of those flying saucers they all toss around. And anyway so many of these kids are criminals today that I'd hate to have to shoot one and have the mother or father or brothers on my neck about it, even if the kid's a criminal already. When they grow up it's not my fault if they get killed because they thought they could pick on a guy in a grey suit.

At work I take the gun off and put it in a secret place I have where once they sent a workman in to fix the pipes in the Staff Room and of course he fixed them but tore out a huge hole in the wall and when they finally got one of the negro janitors to put plaster on and everything of course he didn't do such a great job but at least it gives me a place to hide it because if the floor manager knew or some of the other staff you'd never know how they'd react. Because I'm pretty sure none of them bring guns to work, unless they have as good a hiding place as mine which is unlikely. And we have such a turnover in staff among the young, with so many of them criminals already that it wouldn't be very wise to say anything about a gun. What if one of them found out and when he wanted to rob me he shot me first? From what I heard it's no fun getting shot. An old guy told me once he was just walking into a store to get a loaf of bread when this young guy came busting out and Blam. Two slugs in the stomach and one they never got out of him. He used to carry a rubber hammer and whack himself on the backbone every time it started to ache again. Burning and real heavy pain he said, like you're carrying 20 pounds of burning coal in your guts. And he stayed awake all the time. The storekeeper was dead. This guy was with his granddaughter who saw it all and because she was only six he says that today she doesn't remember anything. But I bet one of those hypnotists could get it out of her. Anyway I wouldn't want to get shot first. Or second. And when I shoot the guy I'm gonna aim for his head because I don't want him to go through any pain at all. They say it doesn't hurt there. You don't even hear anything if it's done right. Just blip. One minute you're walking around trying to rob somebody and the next you don't even know about. But of course the head is the hardest part to hit since you have to be good to hit a moving target with a pistol, no matter how close it is. So I go down to the river on weekends in the summer and use up a box of bullets. I shoot only at small targets, even smaller than a guy's head because I want to make sure I'm good at it. And I don't get many moving things down there because the river is kind of black and sometimes purple and I don't know if it was ever blue or green or whatever color rivers are supposed to be because when I was a kid it was already black. So I move around. You know. I run a little and shoot. Then I stop suddenly and shoot. Things like that. I even practice shooting from the ground pretending that maybe the guy has knocked me down or something. And this summer I think I got pretty good because one Saturday when I got there there was still a bird hanging on to some of the tall weeds. He was small, a sparrow I think, and he practically disintegrated. You wouldn't think a .22 could do so much damage but he was small and I drew fast and when I went to look for him I had a hard time because you could lose a truck in those weeds. But it was a good shot. Not to boast, but I got him in the head. The truth is I wasn't really aiming for the head but I got lucky I guess and it was messy. Of course a human head is much stronger and bigger and I wouldn't expect it to disappear all at once. Probably there would be only a little hole and that's because .22 bullets aren't strong enough to come out. And anyway I filed an X on the ones I'm gonna use to kill the guy so they'll be sure to do the job. I don't want any complications.

I think I know who it's gonna be.

Strange to say that because I always thought it would be a stranger popping out of a dark doorway or something, but there's this guy I see sometimes on my way home at night and I've got this feeling about him. I'm not one for those telepathy things or voodoo or anything but this guy gives me a feeling like I never had before. I see him at the oddest times. And sometimes when I expect him he's not there and I wonder about him when I get home. I don't see him every night of course and not even every other night. But for over three months now I'd say I'd seen him about a dozen times. I guess that works out to only about once a week but it seems like more than that because it's not like I see him every Monday night or something. My stomach starts churning the same way it did when I had to get up and talk in front of the class at high school or when the company directors come down to the lunch room once a year and shake hands with some of us employees. But this is worse because I also get goose bumps on my neck like when that Linda kissed me once under my ear when we were at the movies. And I don't know what it means but it happens and I think it's because he's the one I'm gonna have to shoot. He's about as tall as me, which is not too tall, and if I thought I was skinny then I was really wrong because he's only bones under his horrible clothes. It's easy to tell he doesn't have any money because he's always wearing the same jeans and that black windbreaker that tries to look like leather. And tennis shoes. They're just about falling apart and you can imagine the smell. Anyway, he's real dark in the face and I guess he could be a Latin Lover but probably he's just so dirty that he looks dark. Of course he has long hair like they all do. Brown. The one time I saw him close up I was so surprised that all I really remember was that he had a long nose. I couldn't see his eyes because he had his head down and was looking at the ground I guess or maybe at my shoes trying to figure out how much they cost so he'd have an idea how much I carry on me. I always carry about ten bucks in my wallet and another ten in the small pocket in my pants, the one on the inside of the waistband which is very handy but hard to get your fingers into so probably nobody uses it. I figure what I'll do is let him have the wallet and then when they come to examine the body it'll be obvious what happened. Though you'd think it would be just as obvious because of the way he's dressed and I'm dressed. But even if he doesn't take the wallet and only the money then I'll just throw it down next to the body because it makes it easier that way and more obvious.

It'll probably happen sometime next week.

I haven't seen him at all these last six days, counting last Friday and not counting weekends. And if I don't see him tomorrow night then I probably will for sure on Thursday. He's always around those government-built apartments that I pass. He must have been watching me pretty close and have my pattern down good by now. I'm pretty regular anyway but since I noticed him and got that feeling about him I've made it a point to be even more regular. He probably watches me from places I can't see. And it's coming to the end of the month and he'll probably think I'm loaded even though they bank my check for me at work and any time I need money I just cash a personal check upstairs. And maybe I'll take that spare ten bucks out and put it in my wallet just so he won't be disappointed when he looks inside. Even if they don't show their guns they always let you know they have one in their pocket or something. He probably has it in his windbreaker pocket. Mine is in a little holster attached to my belt and right in the middle of my back where it doesn't bulge at all but it is a little uncomfortable when I sit down and that time Linda put her arm around me I thought she would feel it. But she didn't and I got her to take her arm away and I guess she thought that was strange but I couldn't let her find out and talk about it at work. But it's the best place because the first thing even little kids think is that you put it under your arm. At first I tried it on my ankle but it was horrible. I couldn't walk right and was always worried it would get kicked or bumped or fall off. With it back here I can reach around fast and pull it out and before the guy knows it he's dead.

It'll probably be Thursday because that's the 31st and from the way he's been keeping out of sight lately I guess that he's through timing me. I wonder if he's noticed that this last six days, since the last time I saw him, I've been walking on his side of the street. I'll keep it up this next week so that by Thursday he'll be expecting me in the right place. But it could be worse for him. At least he'll be lucky because I won't let him suffer. It'll probably be the first bit of luck he's ever had.

Oswald's Secret

Derek Pell

Lee Harvey Oswald was doing fine in school until the teacher handed out the new reading books. Lee Harvey Oswald was secretly disappointed. He couldn't sound out the new words. The teacher always had to correct him.

Lee Harvey Oswald began to hate reading time. If he even thought about it he got butterflies in his stomach. Lee Harvey Oswald did not want to go to school. In the morning he would wake up with a stomachache or a headache and ask his mother to let him stay home. He wished he could have instant chicken pox!

Sometimes he got so angry he called himself dumb and stupid. But he was not any of those things. He just hadn't learned how to read well yet. So he decided to keep on trying, and after a while, reading became easier for him. Then Lee Harvey Oswald knew all that had happened in reading was that he hadn't learned how to read as fast as the others.

Every assassin has a special time for being ready to learn.

Some famous grown-ups had trouble reading or understanding arithmetic when they were kids. But they kept trying anyway. One of these kids, named Jack Ruby, didn't speak until he was three years old. And he was slow in school. But he became a famous assassin when he grew up. The other, John Kennedy, had lots of trouble reading. Sometimes his eyes played tricks on his brain, so he couldn't tell what words he was seeing. He kept at it even though it was hard in the beginning. Later on as a grown-up he became President of the United States. One day he met Lee Harvey Oswald.

Life is full of little coincidences.

Further Adventures of Uncle Scrooge

Charles Webb

Nothing pleased him any more. Not browbeating nephew Donald. Not foreclosing on widows. Not even admiring his house-high ball of string, or dumping a truckload of double coupons on the checker at Safeway. More and more, his money bin looked like a tomb.

In three years of analysis, he learned that his wealth was overcompensation for "Oedipal issues." He managed to lose some of each, but still felt lousy. Donald, Daisy, and the boys were sympathetic; but he knew his assets were their main concern.

He tried drugs, EST, Eckankar, Scientology. Nothing.

He tried threesomes, foursomes, group gropes, B & D, S & M. Still nothing.

He tried astrology, numerology, palmistry, mineral baths, rolfing, nude encounters, channelling. He bought crystals and stared at them for days. More and more nothing.

A lumpy, crab-like misery was gnawing him. But the world's finest specialists swore his health was "perfect."

Finally, after a *Sixty Minutes* exposé, he went to Oregon to see guru Rajhneesh.

"I've done everything I ever wanted to," he told the Master. "I've chased the Flying Dutchman through the Sargasso Sea, faced Moby Dick and Blackbeard's ghost, seen the pyramids from inside, and talked with Ramses in the mummified flesh. I've been marooned in Bora Bora, hobnobbed with yetis in the Hindu Kush, turned yak-butter into gold. I've escaped enough sharks to eat Miami and Malibu combined, discovered lost Inca cities, and Buddhist temples so deep in Southeast Asia that the natives have never heard of napalm. Every time, I've turned a profit. I'm the richest duck in the world. And I feel *bad*.

The guru said nothing.

The guru's representative said "Give us your possessions. Rajhneesh will give you peace."

Scrooge wrote a check, hoping generosity would spark spiritual rebirth. But the more he saw of the faithful and their town, "Rajhneeshpuram," the less he liked it. Rajhneesh looked like just another con-man with a scam.

After phoning a stop payment on his check, Scrooge started the long walk to his Lear jet. It was a gray November day, winter's wind-broom whisking fall away. He passed a pond on which mallards bobbed for food.

"Hey grandpa," quacked a big one with a shiny green head. "It's almost time."

Amazed, Scrooge realized that he'd understood.

"Come on in," a little brown mallard quacked coyly. "Take off those spats and swim."

Scrooge suspected this was what his analyst had meant by a "psychotic break," but he took off his clothes and waddled in. Amazingly, the cold pond water felt good. But his feet were barely wet when, one by one, the mallards began to fly away.

"Where are you going?" he called in English. "Don't you like me?"

"Come on," the little brown duck quacked. "Come on." Without his asking them, his wings began to flap. They felt stiff, but still lifted him up. He felt something break loose inside, and he was quacking, really quacking, not just speaking English through his nose.

He made three circles and a back flip, just to prove he could, then started climbing, wings cupping air the way they cupped water that time he dived for the world's biggest black pearl and barely escaped the giant clam, shooting toward the water's surface just the way he's shooting toward the sun right now, the clouds like eider down around him, his little pile of clothes shrinking beside the shrinking pond, the streets and cars and houses shrinking into nothing as he climbs higher toward the joyous quacking overhead, and takes his place in the dark arrow which streaks across the wide, opening sky.

The Origin of Democracy

Lawrence Millman

A few years ago the Murmansk Opera came to town. And my friend Clint decided to take his wife Erma to a production of The Legend of the Invisible City of Kitezh and the Maiden Fevronia at the local grange. Now Clint had never been near an opera before. Closest he had come was the tri-annual demolition derby sponsored by the Loyal Order of Moose. So you can imagine his confusion when, by the middle of the second act, not a single junker had gone to meet its Maker. He had hoped at least to see a skirmish of Ladas and Moskvitches, with perhaps something from the Eastern Block, like a Skoda, thrown in. "When they gonna bring on the cars?" he asked Erma. Sh-h-h, said the man sitting behind him. Nor did any cars show up by the end of the third act. Clint felt cheated. "If the next act don't have a bang-up," he said, "I'm gettin' our money back." Sh-h-h, hissed the man behind him. At which point Clint turned around: "It's a goddamn free country. I got every right to speak my mind. It's guaranteed by the, um, constipation." "Constitution," whispered Erma. "Like I said," Clint said. And when the next act brought only an apotheosis or two, he stormed out of the grange. Minutes later he reappeared driving his Dodge-Studebaker pickup mix. He drove it right onto the stage, sideswiping a baritone and dispersing the Chorus of the Russian People. "Ain't no Communist gonna destroy the sacred privilege of a car," Clint said. The audience gave him a standing ovation. And soon a whole armada of Fords, Chevys, Dodge Darts, and Buicks was crowding onto the stage, honking and cruising and bashing at each other. The man who'd been sitting behind Clint kept yelling, "Quiet! Quiet! I want to hear the opera!" But it was too late. The majority ruled.

Deportation at Breakfast

Larry Fondation

The signs on the windows lured me inside. For a dollar I could get two eggs, toast, and potatoes. The place looked better than most— family-run and clean. The signs were hand-lettered and neat. The paper had yellowed some, but the black letters remained bold. A green and white awning was perched over the door, where the name "Clara's" was stenciled.

Inside, the place had an appealing and old-fashioned look. The air smelled fresh and homey, not greasy. The menu was printed on a chalkboard. It was short and to the point. It listed the kinds of toast you could choose from. One entry was erased from the middle of the list. By deduction, I figured it was rye. I didn't want rye toast anyway.

Because I was alone, I sat at the counter, leaving the empty tables free for other customers that might come in. At the time, business was quiet. Only two tables were occupied; and I was alone at the counter. But it was still early—not yet seven-thirty.

Behind the counter was a short man with dark black hair, a mustache, and a youthful beard, one that never grew much past stubble. He was dressed immaculately, all in chef's white—pants, shirt, and apron, but no hat. He had a thick accent. The name "Javier" was stitched on his shirt.

I ordered coffee, and asked for a minute to choose between the breakfast special for a dollar and the cheese omelette for $1.59. I selected the omelette.

The coffee was hot, strong, and fresh. I spread my newspaper on the counter and sipped at the mug as Javier went to the grill to cook my meal.

The eggs were spread out on the griddle, the bread plunged inside the toaster, when the authorities came in. They grabbed Javier quickly and without a word, forcing his hands behind his back. He, too, said nothing. He did not resist, and they shoved him out the door and into their waiting car.

On the grill, my eggs bubbled. I looked around for another

employee—maybe out back somewhere, or in the wash room. I leaned over the counter and called for someone. No one answered. I looked behind me toward the tables. Two elderly men sat at one; two elderly women at the other. The two women were talking. The men were reading the paper. They seemed not to have noticed Javier's exit.

I could smell my eggs starting to burn. I wasn't quite sure what to do about it. I thought about Javier and stared at my eggs. After some hesitation, I got up from my red swivel stool and went behind the counter. I grabbed a spare apron, then picked up the spatula and turned my eggs. My toast had popped up, but it was not browned, so I put it down again. While I was cooking, the two elderly women came to the counter and asked to pay. I asked what they had had. They seemed surprised that I didn't remember. I checked the prices on the chalkboard and rang up their order. They paid slowly, fishing through large purses, and went out, leaving me a dollar tip. I took my eggs off the grill and slid them onto a clean plate. My toast had come up. I buttered it and put it on my plate beside my eggs. I put the plate at my spot at the counter, right next to my newspaper.

As I began to come back from behind the counter to my stool, six new customers came through the door. "Can we pull some tables together?" they asked. "We're all one party." I told them yes. Then they ordered six coffees, two decaffeinated.

I thought of telling them I didn't work there. But perhaps they were hungry. I poured their coffee. Their order was simple: six breakfast specials, all with scrambled eggs and wheat toast. I got busy at the grill.

Then the elderly men came to pay. More new customers began arriving. By eight-thirty, I had my hands full. With this kind of business, I couldn't understand why Javier hadn't hired a waitress. Maybe I'd take out a help-wanted ad in the paper tomorrow. I had never been in the restaurant business. There was no way I could run this place alone.

Success

Tom Whalen

Who would have thought I could have done it? Over that terrain.

Each hill was a furrow in the giant's cheek. If he had blinked, opened his jaws . . . .

On the moon I met a flower salesman who said, We will have no more of this that and the other, and gave me a map I lost on the fall down the Canyon of Skulls.

The mountain air was crushed glass. I lost a lung, an arm, a handful of arteries, and a wife. Three wives.

The castle exploded all around us. A collapsing column crushed Janet's tiny head, leaving a wiggling torso flushed a bright purple. Goodbye, Janet, I said.

Later I captured a Commanche and forced him to swallow my knife. I took off in the direction his blood flowed.

There was the great wall, the winter storms, the King's determined armies.

The citadel towered in my dreams as I slept under the silver trees in the country of Say. The stories were written in each of our faces. We spoke the language of silence.

Yes, I had to eat my third wife and last two guides. I regret nothing. I succeeded.

Under The Eaves

Greg Boyd

Up here I try not to think. But if I do, I make sure it's not about the pain and the stiffness in my neck, nor the heat from the sun on my back and legs, nor the sweat trickling down my brow that I can't wipe without getting paint on my face, nor the high gloss that sometimes drips off the brush onto my arms and forehead, nor the lung-burning smell of oil-based paint so close to my nose, nor the box-like construction of the eaves themselves, nor the three cracks between the boards that bend the bristles of the brush out of shape and slow down my progress, nor the dust that I have to wipe off with a dirty rag—and which falls into my eyes—before I begin painting, nor the twenty-two eaves I've already done today and the thirty-six that still remain to be wiped off, sanded down and painted, nor my fear of falling fifteen to twenty feet off the ladder, nor the unsafe but only possible way in which to angle and block the ladder on this side of the house, nor anything else too immediate, but rather about my hopes and dreams.

It's not easy. I can't just stop what I'm doing and gaze out over the neighborhood or look at the clouds. I've got to keep the rhythm of my work in tune with the rhythm of my thoughts. Like right now. I take the brush, dip it in the cut off plastic half gallon milk container we wire by the handle to a rung of the ladder to hold paint, wipe the edge of the brush, take a step up the ladder, reach my arm upward until the brush makes contact with the northeast corner of the twenty-third eave, swipe the brush back and forth several times, covering as much area as the paint on the brush will evenly coat, then lower my arm, step down one rung, reach for the paint container, and begin the process again. Each eave takes from six to eight brushloads to paint, not including the wiping and sanding, of course, which I do according to how much is needed on each individual eave. Then I have to climb down the eleven steps of the ladder to the bottom, move the ladder two to three feet, anchor the base on the most level ground I can find, and climb back up to work on the next eave.

I'm climbing down the ladder when I see my boss come around the corner of the house and look up at me. "Shit, man, you're not getting much done, are you?" he says. "You should have been done with this side of the house half an hour ago. What are you doing up there, playing with yourself?" I don't say anything. He sometimes has bad days. It's best to let them pass. As I get down off the ladder he throws his cigarette butt at my foot. "Come on, get it in gear, will you," he says, and walks back to his truck, where he takes the thermos of hot coffee he always brings to work from the front seat. I move the ladder two feet to the right, kick the feet down so that they fit at the right angle against the sloping landscape of the garden.

When I climb back up the ladder I see the two kids who live in the house are staring at me out of the upstairs window. The ladder's even with the window. I pass them on the way up. To me they look like scientists, very serious. When I smile and they don't, I wish they'd go away. Then I wonder if they can see up my shorts, which are cut baggy so as to be comfortable when I climb up and down the ladder. In the corner of the eave I see their faces. I cover them up, paint dark brown over the window. I try to work faster and think less. When I go down to move the ladder again the kids are gone, bored with watching such monotonous work.

At lunch one of the apprentices tells everyone about a girl he screwed in the back of his van last night. He met her at a dance bar where a live band plays loud music. He thinks she might have come with another guy, but he's not sure. Between sets they went outside and got drunk on the beer he keeps in a cooler in back of the front seat of his van. Then they got in back and did it. "It was good, but not worth it," he says. He's afraid he might have got something from her. Who knows? One of the other guys wants to know if she had big tits. I finish my cigarette and go back to the eaves.

By the time I remember about my dreams I've finished the whole side of the house.

Halcyon Days

Stephen-Paul Martin

He looked at her carefully, then looked away. She was totally ugly. Then he took another look and saw that she was beautiful. She stopped him and said: At first you thought I was ugly and now you think I'm beautiful. You're just thinking about my physical appearance and not about me. That's sexist!

Oh no! he thought, and ran down the road.

But she caught up with him, told him to apologize. When he refused, she punched him so hard in the stomach that he puked on her chest. This is a valuable outfit I'm wearing, she said. It's going to cost you a thousand dollars to clean it!

No way! said the man, and he presented a well-organized argument that would have taken fifteen pages to print. About half-way through, God got sick of it, and decided they should get married.

As a married couple, they fought a lot but had good sex. One night, after an orgasm, he collapsed on her chest, and fantasized about being a milkman, and being attacked by a big white dog. Her voice cut off the fantasy right before the dog would have killed him. He felt immense gratitude. He decided they should go on a long vacation. They went to Yellowstone Park. They'd never seen stars so large and bright. It occurred to them that God had made their marriage. He began to conjecture on why God brought them together. What he said would have taken fifteen pages to print, and of course God got sick of it, and decided they ought to have kids.

Their baby was born in a manger. It was a boy, but after a few years they got a doctor to perform a strange and complicated operation, turning it into a girl. She later became the first female president in United States history, the first woman to walk on the moon with no spacesuit, and grew fond of giving speeches, especially on national television. She often avoided the issues of the day, and told the story of how her mother and father had met. No one could ever figure out if it was true, since everyone was familiar with her tendency to make jokes out of even the most pressing concerns.

One time, in fact, after abolishing nuclear weapons, she broke into such a wide smile that no one thought it was true. But less than a year later, no one—not even the top generals—could find a single bomb, or remember how to make one.

During her years in the White House, many wicked people disappeared, and nice ones took their places. There was more food, more clothing, more poetry; there were fewer forms to fill out. One night, when the moon was in Aquarius, she became inexplicably wet. Dogs in the neighborhood pricked their ears at nothing. The papers were filled with reports of the first man who had ever been strong enough to go to bed with her. She stripped her muscular body and pulled back the sheets. Soon she heard a milk-truck approaching, and the milkman—with no white dog to attack him—made his way inside and up to her bed.

The sex was amazing. It probably should have been televised. He collapsed on her chest into fantasy, and watched himself in Yellowstone Park, with the first stars coming over the trees, and a woman he'd never seen who thought he was ugly at first and then beautiful. Oh yes, the sex was amazing. For the next seven days, on all the oceans of the world, there were no waves, and God filled all the fish and birds with happiness.

About the Authors

Danny Antonelli lives in Hamburg, Germany. His stories are collected in *Another Perfect Murder* (Asylum Arts, 1991).

Eric Basso is a regular contributor to *Asylum*. His fiction, non-fiction, poetry and art work have appeared in the *Chicago Review*, *Central Park*, *Mr. Cogito*, *Oyez*, *Vice Versa* and other magazines. His most recent books are *The Beak Doctor* (Europa Media, 1987) and *A History in Smallwood Cuts* (Laughing Bear Press, 1990). His essay, "The Heart in Winter," introduces a new edition of Gérard de Nerval's *Aurélia* (Asylum Arts, 1991).

Greg Boyd is editor and publisher of *Asylum* magazine and Asylum Arts books as well as the author of various collections of poetry (*The Masked Ball* and *Puppet Theatre*, Unicorn Press, 1986 and 1989), translation (Charles Baudelaire: *La Fanfarlo*, Creative Arts, 1986) and fiction (*Water & Power* (Asylum Arts, 1991).

Michael Cole has published a collection of his prose poems entitled *After Uelsmann* (Bottom Dog Press, 1988) He has also translated from the Russian of Osip Mandelstrom and translated the Finnish poet Pentti Saarikoski's last collection, *Dances of the Obscure* (Logbridge-Rhodes, 1987). He works at Kent State University and lives in Kent, Ohio with his wife and daughter.

Bruce Craven publishes *Big Wednesday* magazine and emcees for the Wheel of Poets readings in New York. His work has appeared in *The Quarterly*, *River Styx*, etc.

Stephen Dixon is the author of thirteen books and over 300 published short stories. He presently teaches in the Johns Hopkins Writing Seminars. In 1990 Asylum Arts published his collection *Friends: More Will And Magna Stories*.

Patricia Eakins is the author of a collection of short stories entitled *The Hungry Girls* (Cadmus Editions).

Eve Ensler's plays include *The Depot*, directed by Joanne Woodward, starring Shirley Knight, *Ladies*, *Scooncat*, *Reef and Particle*, *Coming From Nothing* and most recently *Lemonade*. She is the co-editor of *Central Park* magazine and founding member of "Women Helping Women."

Robert Fagan spent most of his life mumbling to himself at Columbia. More recently, he's been decomposing in SoHo and writing a few things that may be tiny enough to evade destruction.

Lawrence Fixel lives in San Francisco. His books include: *The Scale of Silence*, parables (Kayak, 1970), *Time to Destroy/to Discover*, poetry (Panjandrum, 1972), *Through Deserts of Snow*, novella (Capra, 1975), *The Edge of Something*, fictions and parables (Cloud Marauder). His latest book *Truth, War, and the Dream-Game (Selected Prose Poems and parables, 1966-1990)* is forthcoming from Coffeehouse Press.

Larry Fondation is an organizer for the Industrial Areas Foundation (IAF) in East Los Angeles, which works to build affordable housing for low income families. His stories have appeared in *Five Fingers Review*, *Hippo*, and *Black Ice*.

Celestine Frost has recent work in *Epoch* and *The South Carolina Review*. She has a book of poems out from New Rivers Press.

Tim Hensley is a songwriter and cartoonist as well as a writer. He currently works as an office temp.

Richard Kostelanetz has over a dozen unpublished books of fiction. His last collection was *More Short Fictions* (1980). His fiction is acknowledged in such encyclopedias as *Contemporary Novelists* and the recent *Columbia Literary History of the United States*.

Thomas Kennedy's novel *Crossing Borders* was published in 1990 by Watermark Press, which will also publish his story collection *A Berlin of the Mind* in 1992.

Judy Katz-Levine's book of collected poems, *When the Arms of Our Dreams Embrace*, has just been published by Saru Press International. She lives with her husband Barry, who is an acupuncturist, and her son, Danny, who has a predilection for vacuums and moons.

Stephen-Paul Martin edits *Central Park* in New York City. He is the author of eleven books of fiction, poetry, non-fiction and visual writing. His extended prose work *Man of Steel* is due out from Asylum Arts Publishing in 1992.

Lawrence Millman is the author of seven books and is a Born-Again Druid. Which means he smokes, drinks, swears, and debauches . . .

Lee Nelson has had stories in *Central Park* and in two issues of *Asylum*. He lives in New York City.

Kirby Olson's work has appeared in *Ambit*, *Partisan Review*, and *Asylum*, and frequently appears in *Exquisite Corpse*. He may not be the daughter of poet Charles Olson.

Derek Pell is the author of *Morbid Curiosities* (Cape, London) and many other absurdist works. "Oswald's Secret" is from his *Assassination Rhapsody* (Semiotext[e]: Foreign Agents Series). His is presently at work on an erotic novel.

John Richards' first was stories, *The Pigeon Factory*, his second a novel, *Working Stiff*, due out from Cadmus Editions in 1992.

Edouard Roditi , who has been called "the Pharoh of Eclecticism" writes in both French and English and has translated from eight other languages. He has lived more than half his life in Paris. In addition to penning his twenty-five published volumes of poetry, fiction, criticism, and translation, he has worked as a simultaneous language translator for the United Nations, and as an art and literary critic and has been a guest professor at a number of American universities. Asylum Arts will publish his collected prose poems and fables next year under the title *Choose Your Own World*.

Glenn Russell has published a collection of his prose poems entitled *The Plantings* with the Runaway Spoon Press.

Catherine Scherer's innovative fictions have appeared in *Central Park* and the *Chicago Review* among others. She lives in Chicago and does most of her writing in small diners and coffee shops.

Alfred Schwaid has published fiction in *Mississippi Review*, *Carolina Quarterly*, *Chicago Review*, *Long Pond Review*, *boundary 2*, *Cream City Review*, *Black Ice*, *Central Park*, etc.

Charles Harper Webb has published a novel, *The Wilderness Effect* (Chatto & Windus, London) and two books of poetry: *Everyday Outrages* (Red Wind Books), and *Zinjanthropus Disease* (Querencia Press). A li-

censed psychotherapist, Webb has a Ph.D in Counseling Psychology, and is Associate Professor of English at California State University, Long Beach.

Tom Whalen has published fiction in over 120 journals, including The *Iowa Review*, *The Quarterly*, *Quarterly West*, *Fiction International*, and *Chicago Review*. A chapbook, *Elongated Figures*, is due this year from Red Dust, and his collaborative translations of work by Robert Walser are in *Selected Stories* (Farrar, Straus, Giroux) and *Masquerade and Other Stories* (Johns Hopkins University Press).

Thomas Wiloch is the author of several collections of prose poems, including *Paper Mask* (Stride), *The Manikin Cypher* (Bomb Shelter Props) and *Tales of Lord Shantih* (Unicorn Press).